Bill
AND
Olga

A DELMARVA LOVE AND SPY STORY

JAC. K. SPENCE

iUniverse LLC
Bloomington

BILL AND OLGA
A DELMARVA LOVE AND SPY STORY

iUniverse books may be ordered through booksellers or by contacting:

iUniverse LLC
1663 Liberty Drive
Bloomington, IN 47403
www.iuniverse.com
1-800-Authors (1-800-288-4677)

ISBN: 978-1-4917-1577-2 (sc)
ISBN: 978-1-4917-1578-9 (e)

Printed in the United States of America.

iUniverse rev. date: 12/20/2013

Preface

First, let me say I never had an interest in writing a book, or for that matter, even writing a grocery list. When my wife, Mary, and I met a young Russian woman at a Delmarva restaurant by the name of Ekaterina Polyantseva, something clicked and we became instant friends. When she returned to Russia, and invited us to visit her there, we accepted her gracious invitation without thinking twice about it.

When we arrived at Domodedovo International Airport in Moscow she was waiting for us at the welcoming area. From that hour on she became our guide, our interpreter, our everything. We visited cities like Moscow, and St. Petersburg, as well as wonderful mid- sized cities like her home town of Kostroma, and small picturesque villages like Plyos, nestled between a hillside and the Volga River.

Meeting Katerina's mom and dad, Marina and Andrey, was so special. The dinner they served at their comfortable home was delicious and memorable. Kate's friend Anton was a real gentleman and quite handsome as well. And we can never forget Sergei, our taxi driver in Moscow. He was much younger than I but we became soul brothers as we enjoyed his music on our night tours of Moscow.

There were times I would wander off on my own and test Kate's patience but she was always quick to forgive. Kate became the inspiration for me to pick up a pen and use my imagination to write a novel. I hope you enjoy it.

Acknowledgements

I dedicate this book to Ekaterina Polyantseva, a most special lady. She was my inspiration for writing this book and indeed awakening an interest in writing I never realized was present. In fact, I actually loathed picking up a pen to write anything. Also, the desire to visit Russia was always in my blood and Kate made it all happen. Mary and I will never forget you Kate. (I might add that even though Katerina didn't like the name Kate she allowed me to use it since the name reminded me of a princess.)

My thanks to the following people for their advice, interest and patience as I worked through this project of love; My wife Mary, Liudmila Chernova, Vadim Matei, Dasha Sementsova, Vera Petrova, Sergei, (our taxi driver in Moscow), Dr. Bob & Suzanne Mozayeni family, Dick and Elaine Oakes, and Jeff and Lisa Culler.

Also, a special thanks to Helen Stevens for taking my raw and rough manuscript and suggesting ways to make it better which I was happy to implement. To my second cousin, Ron Stevens, for finding and marrying Helen to be here for such an important project all these years later.

The Deception

When Bill retired to the beach, he was intent on doing all the things he didn't have time to do when he ran his small energy related business for over 35 years. It will be all about long walks on the beach, girl watching, gardening, golfing, parties and dining out. He was tired of box lunches and fast food stops, never having the time to relax because every minute of his time had been spoken for and that is the typical life of a small entrepreneur. His long marriage of over three decades to Betsy Bond was terminated in a very friendly and amicable way with Bill insisting that she get the lion's share of their accumulated assets.

To keep himself busy he decided to take some of his funds and begin a one person investment business. This would be a diversion from all his other activities. One of his very favorite past times was to take a lot of reading material to the beach early in the morning before the sun got too hot.

One morning while reading one of his favorite magazines, he come across an article aimed at retirees titled, "six things to do if you want to stay young and at the same time have a more interesting life." There was all the usual advice about diet, exercise and all the rest but what got Bill's attention was "don't be afraid to flirt with the ladies." And he did just that with a zeal and dedication that even surprised him. He was having a lot of fun and most of the ladies went along with his foolishness and he made a lot of friends in the process. Then one warm and sultry evening in the summer of 2010 at Hannah's while dining with friends a beautiful vivacious 23 year old Russian girl by the name of Olga came to their table and she would be their server. To this day Bill could not remember the words he used to get her attention but after a while she seemed to warm to his silliness and despite their age difference there was a chemistry building between them and both sensed they would be seeing each other after tonight. Olga was not only beautiful with a magnetic personality but had a charisma and intellect that made her irresistible to all the guys who were regulars at Hannah's. For Bill, who was decades older, it was love from almost the start and she made him feel young and vibrant again.

Then one day while dining alone, she came to his table and engaged him in conversation and invited him to accompany her on a day's trip to Chincoteague to relax on the beach and walk their popular nature trails. Bill was ecstatic with her offer and said yes without even checking his personal calendar or even knowing what day of the week she had in mind. Chincoteague was a small seaside town on the southern Delmarva Peninsula whose main attraction was the long sandy beach that stretched for miles on the Atlantic Ocean. It was a favorite summertime destination for tourists, beach freaks, surfers and fishermen. The Island was mainly a marshland with forests of pine and cypress and a mecca for exotic birds and wild ponies, a real paradise for nature lovers. Olga loved the entire island because she said it reminded her of her home town of Kostroma, Russia which is situated on the banks of the Volga River.

After a while they enjoyed each other's company so much that every time she had a day off during the entire summer of 2010, he would pick her up at her apartment in Ocean City, load up her beach umbrella, Frisbees and other beach stuff in his sand mobile (beach mobile), and take the 90 minute drive to Chincoteague. Bill considered himself to be the luckiest guy on the planet and he couldn't have been happier. They would usually start their day on one of the nature trails taking pictures of all the species they came across whether the birds, turtles, wild ponies, black squirrels or anything else that crossed their path.

After their hike, it would be about lunch time and they would more often than not scurry over to Maria's for her famous fried chicken. They always rented a room at the local Quality Inn for bath room purposes and to freshen up because neither could tolerate the toilets provided at the beach. The room or bed was never used for any romantic interlude in all their many trips during the summer. He was quite happy just to be with her and didn't want to suggest anything that might be a turnoff, and he was very happy just to receive her warm embraces and kisses, especially at times when she thought he had made a special effort to make her happy. Now, after over a dozen trips to the island that summer, it was almost like a ritual. In the afternoon, they would take the sand mobile to the beach unload her beach umbrella, Frisbees, chairs, etc.

Bill was quite amused with Olga that she would always insist that she would be the one to secure the beach umbrella and attach the Frisbees and she did it with a diligence and preciseness that seemed unusual, but her personality was such he never questioned her about something that seemed very strange to him. The fact that she would never allow the Frisbees to be used for their intended purpose was even funnier but she was a girl with unusual habits and it only added to her appeal.

The summer was about over and as autumn approached, Bill was aware that Olga would have to return to Russia soon because her visa would soon expire. So, as they headed toward Chincoteague on this particular day, he wondered how many more trips they would be taking together and just the thought of not being with her in the future was not something he wanted to face up to, at least for now.

As they made the left turn off Rt. 13, they were passing the Wallops Island top secret military complex as they had done so many times before with all the sophisticated satellite dishes and antennas and then all of a sudden, a thought came into Bill's mind that HIT HIM LIKE A TON OF BRICKS. Was it possible that Olga's beach umbrella could be a sophisticated transponder and her Frisbees transmitters? Was she intercepting all our incoming intelligence transmissions and sending them back to Moscow? Bill was certain his instincts were correct. The little squares in the quilt like design were probably loaded with microchips and of course with Olga being so meticulous and precise when she anchored her umbrella in the sand began to make sense now and there was little doubt in his mind that Olga was a Russian spy. He was little more than her shill, her cover.

A feeling of betrayal emanated from every bone in his body but he was proud of himself for keeping his cool. Although he was deeply hurt by the woman he fell so very hard for, he was determined to be very vigilant and proceed with their usual pattern while trying to keep his spirit high because any let down in his usual upbeat personality would certainly be noticed by Olga. They did all the things they had done in the past and it was now time to go to the beach and when they arrived there it was about 2:30 p.m. They began to unload to do their usual set up when dark clouds started to form in the skies and they looked ominous to put it mildly.

In fact, most beach-goers seemed to understand that this was something much more than your average summer thunderstorm and they loaded up to get off this unprotected island. But this did not deter Olga in the least, as she began to anchor her umbrella in the sand as she had done so many times in the past totally ignoring the angry ocean just a few yards away.

The Big Storm

It was now clear that Olga was on a mission and it was confirmation to Bill that his suspicions were correct. He was going to miss those sand castles she would construct in the sand that brought so many raves from all those who were around them. Yes, it was just another one of her artistic talents. The winds were now getting stronger and it was apparent to him that this was going to be a very dangerous and destructive storm. Now, even Olga seemed to sense the seriousness of the situation as she rushed to take down her umbrella. They were the only two remaining on the beach and when they got into Bill's sand-mobile the roads were covered with debris and torrents of water and now their very lives were in jeopardy because Bill understood that this island was marshland and to challenge Mother Nature was foolhardy.

The road now was barely passable and the torrents of water became full blown flooding and although his sand-mobile was built for rough travel, it was no match for these conditions. There was no chance that they could make it off the island and now Olga realized their plight and seemed almost resigned that it would take a miracle to keep them from being swept into the tidal waters. Then, as all hope was fading, Bill looked to his left and saw a giant cypress that he remembered guarded the entrance to the historic lighthouse on the hill. When it was constructed in 1867, they made a manmade mountain so the lighthouse would be visible to the seamen of that era. Their only chance of survival was to get to the top of that hill. Could Bill's sand-mobile pull them through another tight situation one more time? The entrance road was blocked by a fallen tree branch and if he had the strength to move it out of the way, they had a chance to escape their dire circumstances. Olga wanted to help but the winds were strong and Bill was afraid they would blow her away. Bill could pull it for a few inches, but not enough to allow his sand-mobile to get by. Then, as he gave it one more try, it began to move. Had God intervened to save them? Not this time, because Olga got out of the vehicle without Bill's knowledge and provided the extra lady-power to get it out of the way and now his sand-mobile could make it past the first hurdle.

Although Bill had to get out several times to move smaller objects, they were moving to higher ground albeit at a snail's pace. As they rounded the last curve, the silhouette of the lighthouse could be seen through his high beams and knowing it was still standing gave both a feeling of comfort because over the 143 year history, it had no doubt seen a few similar storms that matched this one in fierceness.

As Bill turned off his engine, Olga put her arms around him, "Hold me tight Bill, we need each other." Needless to say, he was embracing her tightly because they both were grateful for the efforts expended by each, and Bill was especially thankful for her courage when without him knowing, she got out of the sand-mobile to assist him in moving the big branch off the entrance. By this time, they were both worn out and actually fell asleep huddled together. They had lost all track of time and when Bill awoke it was apparent that this monster storm was subsiding as the winds lessened and the sky began to brighten. She was still asleep in his arms but he noticed her beach blouse had become unbuttoned and her breasts were within inches of his lips. When her eyes opened, Bill being the gentleman as always spoke these words, "Allow me to button you up." She gave him a kiss and then, "Not just yet Bill, they are yours." In his younger years, his instincts would have pushed him into a heated rush, but not now. He wanted every touch, every kiss, every caress to be delivered with tender loving care and this was no time to rush. With just those seven words, Bill could feel the rush of blood to every part of his body.

So, he gently kissed her forehead and lips when she made this suggestion, "We are still sandy from the beach and are in tight quarters and maybe we should try to get to the Quality Inn." They had always reserved a room there in the past for bathroom purposes and to freshen up. This made sense and since they had it reserved until noon tomorrow and it was only a few miles away, they started up the sand-mobile and headed down the hill slowly and from time to time, they both had to get out and clear debris and when they got to the bottom, the water on the road had subsided enough to proceed slowly to the Quality Inn.

It took them about 30 minutes and now they were here, and Olga asked Bill to use the bathroom first and after taking a shower and shave, he slipped under the light cotton sheet in the king size bed and waited for Olga. After what seemed like forever, she emerged from the bathroom in lingerie of bright red and blue trim and now he understood what Aphrodite, the Goddess of Love, must have looked like. Except, Olga, was not an image born out of the waters of the Aegean Sea. She was real and she was Russian who without a doubt are among the most beautiful ladies on the planet. She slipped under the sheet with him and her perfume must have been made from the passion flower because it was intoxicating.

Bill understood all too well that the freedom she extended to him with her body and the pleasures she provided to him would not have been possible without the raging storm that steamrolled across the peninsula. She was showing her appreciation for what they had endured together over the past few hours. Of course she did not know that he was aware her beach umbrella and Frisbees were sophisticated spying devices.

As they drove away from Chincoteague the next morning, Bill understood he had some crucial decisions to make. Prior to the storm and what happened last night at the Inn, he was going to alert the FBI about his suspicions and if they confirmed what he had discovered, she would be sent to the holding facility at the CIA complex in Langley, Virginia. It was said that the holding facility was as comfortable as a five star hotel and maybe she would be released in some future spy-exchange program, but he could not stand the thought that she would not be free. After their near-death experience during the storm and their time in bed, he was now hopelessly in love and for her to be detained for even a minute was something he could not tolerate.

Bill had grown up in a small coal mining village in Western Pennsylvania where country, family and honesty were drilled into every school child from the first grade on. But now, his overwhelming love for Olga had transcended all these early values and now he was ready to stake his life if necessary to see she got home safely to her family and friends in Russia. The 90 minute drive back to her apartment passed quickly and they agreed to meet for dinner before her trip back to Russia, which was now just a fortnight away.

The next several weeks would be a defining period in Bill's life. Olga had enriched his life and all those who knew her because her upbeat personality just lit up the room but before long she would be boarding an Aeroflot plane that would take her to Moscow and maybe he would never see her again. But before her departure they would be having dinner together and since she was still working at Hannah's he would go by to at least see her if nothing else. Just getting a glimpse of her as she scurried about in her white shredded shorts gave Bill goose bumps.

And like a love sick teenager, he made the trip to Hannah's five times during that two week period. But now the evening for their dinner engagement had arrived, and needless to say, he was excited and nervous. To relax, he decided to take the scenic route to her apartment through the Assawoman Wildlife Reserve. It was an area he knew very well as he had taken many walks through its hidden trails since his retirement. The serenity and solitude of the woods and the chirps and noises of all the wildlife provided a sense of calm and humility from the hectic pace of life just a few miles away.

And Bill, through a self-hypnosis process, had convinced himself that Olga was not a spy. As he got closer to her apartment, his mind shifted to their last night together at Chincoteague. He had a guilt complex because he understood she had given herself only because of the ordeal they had endured together. Nevertheless, he would not forget the exhilaration he felt that night and given another opportunity to be with her in that setting tonight after dinner was a tantalizing thought.

Dinner with Olga and a Banana Split

As he pulled into the parking lot of her apartment building, the anticipation he was feeling was indescribable and as he sat there waiting for her, he began to wonder if she would even show up. Maybe his entire experience with her was just a dream but then, there she stood, almost like she appeared from a heavenly cloud in a black mini-dress and red sweater and without a doubt, she was the most glamorous, the most spectacular woman he had ever laid his eyes on.

She gave him a warm hug and kiss and now the evening was underway. For Bill, it was truly a night that dreams are made of but, in many ways it was bittersweet because after tonight he would not see her again because the next day she would be flying back to Russia. To be together as long as possible, Bill asked if they could go to a restaurant he was familiar with in a small eastern shore town about 50 minutes away and she agreed, expressing her wishes to spend more time with him.

During the drive there, as usual, Olga got the conversation going by asking who the people were with him the evening she first came to their table at Hannah's, and he remembered it was his good friends Dr. Bob and Suzanne Moser and their two children Soren and Maggie. Dr. Bob was engaged in a research project to discover better ways to treat the psychological problems of returning soldiers from the battlefield. In fact, that was the subject they were discussing the night Olga appeared at their table.

But this was another night and the 50 minute drive went by quickly and now they were pulling into the parking space of the quaint little

Italian restaurant and when they entered every eye was on Olga and everyone had to be wondering how this old guy got so lucky. Olga, who was the epitome of self-confidence and grace, didn't give a hoot what they may have been thinking and she took complete charge when the waiter appeared at their table. She ordered a bottle of California chardonnay and their house salad, mixing it herself and asking for a more generous portion of their special dressing and their waiter understood that she was in charge and his only job was to deliver whatever they ordered. It was really amusing to watch her performance and the tables close by were getting a big kick out of her antics and no doubt they had also fallen in love with her Russian accent as Bill had when he first met her. Just listening to her voice was enough to want to get her into some romantic setting.

After dinner while walking out, she was given a respectful round of applause by the patrons because she had really created a delightful ambiance and they were showing their appreciation. She acknowledged their applause by giving everyone a gracious smile and wave as they walked out the door. Bill was as proud as a peacock that she was in his company.

On their drive back to her apartment, they passed a Quality Inn and in a teasing voice, she whispered, "Look Bill, that motel reminds me of the one we stayed in at Chincoteague after the big storm." Almost immediately, he thought it was an invitation to turn back and there was no doubt he was ready because the flow of blood had already circulated to the important part of his body. She understood her words had aroused his hormones and when she placed her hand on his inner thigh, she continued, "I'm sorry Bill, I should be more careful with my words but tonight is not a good night for me. But, if you visit me in Russia, there will be ample opportunities to be together in any setting you choose." When he heard that tantalizing offer, he knew he would need to start planning a visit there.

The evening was about over but before going to her apartment she wanted to stop at the Dairy Queen for a banana split. Of all things, another Russian girl was working there and they exchanged pleasantries in Russian smiling and looking at Bill on one of their exchanges. Not having any idea what they had said to each other, he could only hope it was complimentary or maybe they had noticed the bulge near his groin area because he was still feeling the effects of her hand movements around that area during their drive back.

She ordered one banana split and one spoon and as they sat down to enjoy, she would alternate a spoonful of the delicious treat first to his lips and then to hers each time taking her tongue to lick her lips to arouse Bill even further. After dessert, he drove her back to her apartment where they hugged and kissed. She put her hand on it and asking Bill again to visit her in Russia where she would take care of all his personal needs as she had done at Chincoteague. With that, she took a card out of her purse and gave it to him and now their night was over.

When he arrived home and opened the card she had given him, after reading her words, he now understood how much he was going to miss her. She included her e-mail and home addresses, as well as her telephone number, but he knew he had to give her time to readjust to the homeland she had left 16 months earlier. Her birthday was less than a month away and he would use that opportunity to send her a gift to see if she would respond. But the wait was turning out to be a lonely one, so he decided to go over to Hannah's to talk to Svetlani Cheranova, a mutual friend of Olga who worked there while going to school at a local college in hopes of landing a job one day as a broadcast journalist. She was also Russian and was from the city of Tambov, about 400 kilometers south of Moscow.

Like Olga, she was warm and affectionate, always making you feel as if you were the most important guy in the place. She was smart and along with her drop-dead good looks and warm personality, she made you feel better by just being in her company. He knew the time between lunch and dinner, she could sit down and take a break and that is when he went to visit her. She had heard from Olga and she was adjusting well, dating a few of her pasts, although none fit her standard of being "the man of her dreams." Of course, he understood that at his age, he didn't fit that standard either, but she seemed eager for him to visit her in Russia with promises to take care of his personal needs and that was good enough for him.

Before leaving, Svetlani always gave him a heartfelt hug and kiss and in her kidding way, told him that she was in love with him too. Of course, when she added the 'too,' she must have thought that Olga had expressed similar sentiments, although Bill could never remember her saying those words.

As he drove away from Hannah's, he began to think of what Svetlani had told him about Olga dating a few of her pasts, and he began to wonder if they were casual or intimate meetings when all of a sudden, a feeling of jealousy came over him. Yes, she had the right to date anyone she wished and it was none of his business, but after their near-death experience at Chincoteague, he thought a bond had developed between them and somehow, they would be inexorably linked for the remainder of his life.

Doctor Scott's Advice

Of course, this was selfish thinking on his part because she was young and he was old but for whatever reason, a feeling of despondency had crept into his mind and he began to wonder if he could ever survive without her. He understood that he needed help so he contacted a young psychologist by the name of Dr. Erin Scott. She was the daughter of Jeff and Lisa Scott who lived right across the street from him. She had married a terrific young man who Bill knew only as Arnie who had a reputation of attacking the golf course with a daring similar to the king and of course that would be Arnie Palmer from Latrobe, PA. He had watched this beautiful girl grow up and when she married Arnie, he was at their wedding.

But now, she was a professional psychologist and he wondered if she had the time to even listen to him. He decided he would first ask Lisa and Jeff if they thought if it was even proper to ask her but they both agreed it would be a good idea and they volunteered to help arrange a meeting. As it turned out, she was not only willing to accept the challenge, but would be looking forward to the meeting enthusiastically and the appointment was set for a week from today. Now Bill thought that there was someone that would be sympathetic to his condition. Yet he would be a little embarrassed by some of the things he would have to reveal to her but she always had a gift that made everyone feel at ease in her company. And it was that gift that made her so popular with both the young and elderly residents in the neighborhood.

The week went by quickly and when the time came for his appointment, Erin wanted an environment that Bill was comfortable with, so when she informed him she would come to his house, he assumed that the interview would be conducted in the sun room so he made sure there was an assortment of snacks and drinks. When she knocked on his front door, he invited her in. "No, Bill, let's get in your sand-mobile, and I want you to drive us to the place where you feel more comfortable and where we can have some privacy."

This took Bill by complete surprise and he assumed it would have to be in a location not too many miles away and his immediate thought was a place he had grown to love where nature was in all its glory, a very private spot in the Assawoman Nature Reserve. He told her it would be about a 20 minute drive and gave her a brief description of what to expect letting her know that it was fully populated with creatures of nature. "Let's go." was her response and off they went. She had no notebook, no cell phone, and no texting device and Bill thought this was very unusual but when she explained she wanted no interruptions, he understood the kind of atmosphere she was trying to create. When they arrived, it didn't take her long to get down to business.

"Now Bill, I know you have always been a fun guy and my parents and I always enjoyed being in your company, but I want to get serious, because it is obvious that you have been smitten by this young woman from Russia in a way that is causing you great mental anguish and anxiety. I know this because you are not the type to seek help for anything, and the fact that you asked for my help let me know that you need a treatment program." Dr. Scott continued, "I want to help you but you must be candid with me and I must insist that you tell me everything about your relationship with her. Don't leave anything out, and if you had sex with her I want to know all the intimate details. You won't embarrass me and I will keep everything strictly confidential."

Wow!!! This young woman he watched grow up across the street had become an accomplished professional and she was not going to accept anything but the unvarnished truth. So, for the next 90 minutes, he told her the entire story regarding all the trips they made together to Chincoteague in the summer of 2010 and how on the day of the great storm, with their very lives in the balance, they became one and it turned into a romantic interlude at the Quality Inn once they were out of danger. In bed that evening all their emotions spilled over into a variety of touching and oral love that could never be explained by words alone. He went on to tell her about their dinner the last night before her departure for Russia and how their shared banana split and the licking of her lips with her tongue was a big turn on for him. Bill chose not to tell her about his suspicions of Olga being a spy since he had all but wiped it from his mind through a self-hypnosis process.

When Bill finished, Dr. Scott commended Bill for his honesty and willingness to include everything although it was very uncomfortable for him at times. As they drove out of the forest, she explained to Bill that she would send a written evaluation to him in about a week, "But in the meantime, find another woman quickly, preferably another Russian one, because it is obvious that just her very voice excited you." It was true that he loved to hear Olga's voice and he was captivated by the Russian language but needless to say, he was stunned by Erin's recommendation to find another woman quick. She ended the session with this thought, "I know I surprised you with my initial evaluation but when you read my report in the entirety, you will better understand why I believe there is logic in my thinking."

For a few days, Bill was in a state of disbelief and he certainly respected her credentials but taking such a radical step at this time didn't make sense to him. He would consider it a betrayal of Olga and all that had transpired between them would have little meaning. If she didn't respond to his overtures on her birthday, maybe the option of finding someone else would be a more viable alternative but nonetheless, he would be on the lookout to show Dr. Scott he respected her advice and in case Olga decided to end a relationship that seemed so meaningful.

He would keep her advice on the back-burner for now and play a wait and see game, because now enough time had elapsed since Olga's return to Russia and now it was time to send her a birthday gift. Bill sent out a card and gift with a guarantee from Federal Express that she would receive it on November 1 the day of her birth 24 years ago. The distance between Delmarva and Kostroma, Russia seemed like light years away, but now it was time to test his patience. Would he ever hear from her or had she already found that handsome, intelligent guy, "the man of her dreams?" A few days after sending Olga the card and birthday gift, he decided to take the 90 minute drive to Chincoteague to re-visit some of the places he spent so much with Olga. It was late October and the weather was cool but the sun was out in all its glory. Indeed, it was a fantastic time of the year when all the trees would be turning into the colors of autumn. And these colors of autumn were so brilliant it was as if they had set the forest on fire. It was hard to pick a favorite but the maples with their many hues of red would probably be near the top of his list if he was forced to make a choice. When he took that left off Rt. 13, heading toward Chincoteague, it brought back all the memories from the summer that was now over.

When he approached the Wallops Island Military Complex, Bill wanted to forget that flashback on the day they approached the island for the last time. All that followed on that day would affect him for the rest of his life. He decided to go right to the beach and when he arrived he could not believe the number of people that were there this late into the season and no wonder because it was a delightful October day.

Bill could not help but notice a young girl constructing a sand castle in the sand just as Olga had done so many times before. Tears began to form in his eyes, and before anyone could notice, he walked to his sand-mobile and drove down the road that almost ended in a tragedy for him and Olga just one month ago. He stopped his vehicle and walked up the hill to the lighthouse that was truly a beacon of hope that day. Before leaving the site, he gave it a salute not only for him and Olga, but for all the others that might have been saved since it was constructed in 1867. As he drove out of Chincoteague, the memories of Olga consumed his thoughts. When he got home and pulled into his driveway, he noticed that Federal Express had delivered an envelope with the sender's name clearly visible. It was from Dr. Erin Scott and it would be her full evaluation report. But it was a long day so he decided to wait until morning to read and study it so he could give it his full attention when he was rested and alert. All he wanted to do for now was to shower and retire for the evening.

Before going to bed for this evening he decided to check his electronic mail and he couldn't believe what he was looking at. On his screen was the name Olga Kornakova. Like a school kid who just got all A's he kept jumping in the air repeating her name, thanking Olga for being in my life. She did remember him, and again invited him to come to Russia where they could do some things they didn't have quite enough time for when she was in the USA. He thought about their last evening together when she teased him with little short phrases like "Come to Russia and I will take care of all of your needs."

She thanked him profusely for the nice card and gift and promised to stay in touch. He was so happy now, and all of a sudden he was no longer tired. He opened up Dr. Scott's report and it was well written. He was sure her advice was sound but he couldn't act on any of it until he learned more about Olga's intentions. He gleaned from Svetlani that Olga had been dating two of her pasts since returning to Kostroma, and she was well within her right to do so and…of course Bill, if he so desired, could take a lady out to dinner or maybe take it a little farther if the opportunity presented itself.

He couldn't seem to erase from his mind the thought that because of what happened at Chincoteague they would always be together; not to marry necessarily, because it wouldn't be fair to her, but to be soul partners instead, whatever that means. For now he wanted to travel to Russia to see her, and he knew it would take some planning. He would have to update his passport, acquire a Russian visa, make plane and hotel reservations, etc etc. All of this would take time, and since it was already November and the Russian winters are known to be very cold he made the decision to wait until spring.

He looked at his new 2011 calendar and chose May 5th, as his departure date and May 6th to arrive in Moscow. Yes, it was over 6 months away but it would be a test for Olga to see if she felt the same way when he arrived.

An Afternoon with Delilah

The holiday period was just around the corner and Bill was in a celebratory mood. Olga was back in his life so he invited eight of his close friends for dinner at Marty's House of Great Food. It was the place to go not only for great food, but the lively and friendly atmosphere, and the scenic view of the Bay. Bill had been there many times before and the manager set up a beautiful walnut round table as a special favor; life was really good.

It was a wondrous late autumn day and a perfect view of the Bay with just enough sunlight remaining to see the sunset in the western sky in all its glory. When the server arrived in her shimmering long dress, Bill knew he had seen her before. Of course it was a few years back when she worked at a popular breakfast and lunch café called Frenchie's. Almost instinctively he remembered her not by name, but by the number 86. She was a Steelers fan, and it was the number of Hines Ward, her favorite player. She was an 18 year old beauty then, but now after three years she was a gorgeous young woman. She turned out to be an excellent server, and she took all the flirting from the guys at the table in stride, giving each one a wink and a smile.

She was a huge hit, and Bill gave her a 50% tip. As they were leaving, she walked over to Bill and thanked him for the nice tip and at the same time she slipped a note in his hand. He was hoping no one noticed, because she did it in such a stealthy way that he knew it was for his eyes only. He discreetly slipped it into his pocket, and would wait until he arrived home to read it.

When he got home and opened the note, he read these words, "Dear Bill, when are you going to take me out? I guarantee you will not be disappointed. Love, Delilah (aka #86)." She also included her e-mail address.

A few weeks passed since he had been handed the note but his only thoughts during that time were of Olga. Most guys would have contacted her the following day because she was not only beautiful, but had all the body parts to match. One evening, while feeling lonely, he remembered that Dr. Scott advised him to go out and find another lady, preferably a Russian lady. Well, Delilah wasn't a Russian woman, but she made a great substitute.

May 5th was still months away. Since Olga was spending time with her pasts, what would it hurt if he contacted Delilah and see what she was up to? He was in need of a woman for companionship and maybe they could go out to dinner and he could steal a hug and kiss. So, he decided to e-mail her and invite her out to lunch and he got an immediate response. "I don't work tomorrow and I know a nice little French restaurant out in the country that you will love." This was happening a lot faster than he imagined, but why not? So, he met her the next day at a location she had chosen and as they began the drive, it didn't take them long to get off the main road and on to the country road that would take them to the Café Francois which he had never heard of. How could anyone even find this place because now it was nothing but a dirt road without any traffic in either direction? Was there really a restaurant out here or did she have something else in mind when she whispered, "Can I touch you Bill?" To not understand the full implication of that question would be the height of naiveté. Without really thinking, he answered almost casually with, "I guess it will be o.k." With that, she took her left hand and placed it there while removing his right hand from the steering wheel and guided it to her inner thighs.

Then, in the distance, a structure was in sight and he was hoping it was a motel because he was more than ready for the next logical action. But as they got closer, it was a café and as they pulled into the parking lot, she gave him a kiss and, "Let's get a bite to eat. After that, I know a nice place to go just a few miles from here, where I will live up to the guarantee I promised you in the note I gave you at Marty's." There was little doubt that Delilah was a most desirable woman not only with her good looks and beautiful body but also her words and teases to get you ready for what was to follow. Just before getting out of the vehicle to go inside, she whispered, "I was very impressed with what I felt under my left hand and I can't wait to please you in every way." With those words, they entered the Café and without a doubt, with its décor and lighting, it was a place designed to get you in the mood. It was a little dark to guard your privacy no doubt but the candle at each table provided ample lighting to peruse their menu. There were about a dozen couples sprinkled throughout but trying to identify any of them would be difficult even if they were someone you were acquainted with. It was obvious that Delilah had been here on other occasions. Bill was not familiar with their offerings and asked Delilah to recommend an entrée and whatever the concoction was, it was delicious beyond description. The accompanying French wine was all they needed to make their meal complete.

When they got into Bill's sand-mobile to go to the venue where Delilah promised to take care of his needs, all of a sudden, Bill was feeling guilty and was no longer in the mood to continue the destination she had in mind and instead informed her he was going to take her back to her apartment. Delilah could not believe or understand why he had a change of mind, thinking that the strategy she employed was sufficient to get and keep any man in the mood for whatever time was necessary to complete her mission.

Bill began to explain his love for Olga and thought it would not be proper to be in bed with her when his mind was on Olga. Surprisingly, Delilah was very understanding, feeling that if he loved a woman that much she respected him for being honest and forthright. He apologized to her for allowing it to go as far as it did but trying to resist her initial overture at that moment seemed beyond his control. As they got closer to her apartment, it was obvious she had something on her mind other than the aborted tryst. "Bill, I would love to ask a favor of you. I have suffered a temporary financial setback and I won't try to explain how I got myself into this situation except to say it has everything to do with my mother being hospitalized. To get her the treatment she required, I had to exhaust my $1100.00 account to initiate the procedure." Bill took out his checkbook and asked her how much she needed and wrote out a check for a thousand dollars more than she requested. He made sure she understood it was a gift and no payback would be necessary. With that, they hugged and their afternoon together was over.

On his drive back home, his mind was on his close encounter with Delilah and he vowed never to allow himself to be in the company of Delilah in the future because of her obvious sexual attractiveness and persuasive tactics might be too difficult to resist in the future. He had accomplished what Dr. Scott recommended for therapy, "Go out and find another woman and do it quickly." Of course, Delilah was not a Russian woman and why she added, "Preferably a Russian woman" was not clear to Bill but being a psychologist she no doubt had her own good reason.

Svetlani's Invitation

Svetlani Cheranova was Russian but being she was a mutual friend of both Olga and Bill, he always considered her to be untouchable outside her work place at Hannah's. Her and Olga had worked there together for many months and become very close but when Olga went back to Russia, she made it clear to Bill that she would be jealous if their friendship extended beyond the confines of Hannah's. Why Olga felt this way was not clear at the time. Since his trip to Russia was getting closer, he decided to go over to Hannah's to consult with Svetlani and get her advice on what to expect generally when he visited her country. Svetlani was a real sweetheart with a personality that exuded warmth and sincerity.

After Olga went back to Russia, Bill would always request for Svetlani to be his server whether dining alone or with others. All those who met her were smitten by her gentle demeanor and drop dead good looks. But Bill knew that this lady had an unwavering determination to achieve her goals. She was a workaholic doing double shifts at Hannah's while attending a local college and doing an internship at a news outlet. Bill and Svetlani had common interests in that they were both big hockey fans… her favoring the Washington Capitals where the Russian star Alex Ovechkin played and Bill liked the Pittsburgh Penguins where Sidney Crosby and Evegeni Malkin demonstrated their skills. Svetlani hoped her job at the news outlet would be a good way to start a career in broadcast journalism. This would be a great challenge since many news organizations were cutting back on staff and if there were new hires, they would be mostly graduates from the more prestigious universities.

She had amassed an album with stories she had written and entrusted it to Bill for his opinion and critique.

It was easy for Bill to recognize that she was a very talented lady, with both the conviction and perseverance to one day succeed in whatever endeavor she chose. But right now Bill needed her calm disposition and reassuring words before embarking on his trip, now less than a month away.

He was trying to summon the courage to ask her to accompany him for a day trip to Chincoteague where they could relax and discuss not only his Russian adventure, but other topics of mutual interest. Of course this was selfish on his part, considering her busy schedule. On the other hand it might be a nice diversion from the day to day responsibilities, and perhaps provide a fresh perspective that would help her better determine the future of her career.

So, that Friday he decided to get her a gift for her birthday and leave it with a girl they both knew, with an invitation included. Her birthday had already passed, so it would be a belated one, but at least she would know that he had remembered. Bill knew she would be working on Sunday and decided to go there around 3pm since most of the servers would be taking a break between lunch and dinner hours.

When he arrived on that day, Svetlani greeted him with a big smile, but gave no indication whether she had even received the gift and invitation. After giving her his lunch order, he was almost certain a rejection was in store for him. Then, almost without warning, came the words, "Thanks so much for the matching necklace and ear rings. I would be happy to go with you to Chincoteague on Wednesday and with Thursday being a Russian holiday, we could make it an overnighter." Bill's intention was for a one day drive down and back, having time for beach and nature walks and a meal or two at his favorite venues. When she invoked the word overnighter, he understood the implications.

Although taken by surprise, he kept his cool and gave this response, "Great I will pick you up at your rental unit at 9:00 Wednesday morning." And when he had finished his lunch, she gave Bill his usual hug and kiss and this time, her affection seemed more intense than on previous occasions.

When he arrived home, he called to reserve two rental cabins close to each other. Up to this point in their friendship, they understood that any feelings they had for each other would be difficult to manage considering their mutual friendship with Olga. But Svetlani was an independent woman and she didn't mind expressing herself in whatever way she saw fit. To be with her for two days and in less than a month, be with Olga, are what old guys can only dream of because these ladies are exceptional.

The wait from Sunday to Wednesday seemed like forever, but when he arrived at her flat at 9am, she was already outside and with her red and white beach ensemble, she looked spectacular. As they began their 90 minute drive to Chincoteague, the anticipation of what might happen beyond the usual activities there was left only to his imagination. On the way down, they discussed what Bill might encounter while traveling inside Russia and she pointed out that prostitution and robbery were not uncommon in some parts of Moscow and St. Petersburg as well as other mid-sized cities like Tambov which was her home.

When they arrived, they checked into their respective cabins and she did a quick change into her jeans, strapped on her camera and binoculars and headed to the bike rental location. Bill followed with a supply of water and some light snacks. Almost instinctively, she seemed as if she knew where she wanted to go and what she wanted to do. Surely, she must have been here before, but Bill was not about to ask her about any previous trips. She began to lead Bill to places on the Island that were new to him. The pictures she was getting were impressive and for a girl who was working so diligently to achieve her goals, this was the sort of outing she needed. This would be a good lesson for any workaholic.

The day was going by so quickly and although they had water and snacks, they were not enough to satisfy their appetites because their energy requirements were such that only a solid meal would suffice so they biked over to Roy's Shanty, after which they went over to their cabins to freshen up before heading for the beach. They parked their bikes and got into Bill's sand-mobile for the two mile ride because it was already 6pm, and they positioned their chairs at first facing the ocean, and then when the sun set in the western skies, they reversed them because without a doubt it was a magnificent sunset. The planet earth was a special star in the galaxy and for an old guy to be sitting next to this Russian beauty is all that he could wish or ask for. And when the last vestiges of the sun disappeared over the horizon, they picked up their chairs and headed for their favorite ice cream venue on Maddox Street.

Instead of a regular dinner, they both decided on a steak sub and a light beer at the local pub. While there, Svetlani showed Bill all the pictures she had taken. When she got to the one showing two giant turtles mating, she made that one her favorite and said that when she returned home, she would have it framed and placed on her mantel. By this time, they were both dead tired so they decided to retire. As they walked toward their respective cabins, they hugged and kissed and both agreed it had been quite a day. She opened the door to her cabin, and as Bill walked toward his, he heard a familiar voice "And Bill, if you get lonely tonight, I will be here for you."

Wow! Those were words he never expected to hear and when he opened his door to walk in, he was shaking like a leaf in a brisk wind. After all, this was Olga's good friend and he wondered if there had been some disagreement between them. Svetlani was such a sincere and unpretentious person and he could only guess what she might be thinking. Nevertheless, he decided to take a hot shower and then lay down to let it all sink in. Normally, as tired as he was, he would be asleep in minutes but her words kept racing through his mind and sleep was not going to be a viable option. "And Bill, if you get lonely tonight, I will be here for you." was all he could absorb. If he decided to go over to her cabin and Olga found out, would she ever speak to him let alone be his traveling companion in Russia?

It was a dilemma for sure but on the other hand, this was precisely what Dr. Scott had recommended as a therapy for his condition which was an acute case of loneliness. And although that was all before Olga had written to him, he considered it to be a valid option until he could join her in Russia. Bill had now lost all comprehension of time and when he looked at the digital clock on his dresser, it read 11:20pm. He decided to throw caution to the wind and walk over as he threw his night shirt over his Hanes underwear and knocked at her door. As she stood there in her white linen negligee and with her sexy Russian accent she whispered, "I have been expecting you, Bill."

By this time, he was almost trembling from the excitement he was feeling. From now on, whatever happened would be strictly up to Svetlani because he was helpless to resist even if he was inclined to do so. He always took pride in the fact that he never forced himself on any woman, and because he had such a high regard for Svetlani, any act of love would have to be her initiative.

They were still in a tight embrace when Bill realized that anatomically, it was too early into whatever was to follow. If the evening was to have any longevity, there would need to be a pause. Svetlani seemed to recognize his dilemma and made this suggestion, "My mother sent me a bottle of Russian champagne with her last package. I have it with me, so why not take a few minutes to have a glass and converse about all the nice things we did today."

Needless to say, he thought this was a great idea to not only help him relax but to give him more time to be with her before any premature release. So, in her cool and deliberate way, she poured two glasses. As they slowly sipped their portions, he began to feel more confident that he could handle what was coming with a degree of unhurried humility because instead of feeling guilty, he was grateful to her for giving him the opportunity to be with her. From the time they left her flat until now, it had been an enjoyable day and evening. She again showed him a few of her favorite nature pictures and she again mentioned the one of the two turtles mating in the mud was one worthy of a special frame.

The champagne had certainly had its effect on Bill as he was beginning to feel very amorous sitting on the edge of her bed, he took both her hands and pulled her toward him. She had slipped off her negligee and she looked like the perfect model in her pink and white panties and bra. "Take them off for me."

He was glad to oblige, kissing her vulva as he removed her panties and caressing her breasts using his lips and tongue to tease her nipples as they began to harden. Svetlani had also gotten in the mood as she moved her tongue and mouth to every part of his body taking a short break to ask Bill,

"Do you intend to tell Olga that we spent the day and night together at Chincoteague?" After taking a few seconds to think about it, he responded, "Yes, I will tell her we were here but we had separate cabins."

Svetlani was now showing her mischievous side and after getting a big laugh from his timid response, she got back to what she was doing at which time Bill had a full release after which he felt as if this was as close to a heavenly event as one could possibly imagine.

It was like the grand finale at a fireworks display. It was pure ecstasy and as they fell asleep in a warm embrace, Bill understood that this lady was the most passionate woman he had ever been with. When he awoke the next morning, her digital read 11am with just one hour to check out. He heard the shower running and when he peeked in she grabbed it carefully and started to pull him toward her smiling all the while. When she released her handle, they soaped each other down and dried each other off and now it was check-out time. On the way back home when traffic wasn't too heavy, they would play little games of touch. It reminded Bill of his time with Delilah in his sand-mobile heading toward the Café Francois. They were both a little hungry and Bill remembered the café wouldn't be too far out of the way, so before taking her to her flat, they finished their wonderful two days together with some French cuisine and wine. It was a great time for the French in all its meaning. Dr. Scott was absolutely right because this Russian woman is what he needed because now he couldn't be happier.

Bill Travels to Russia

As the days went by, he realized the month of April was almost over, and on May 5th he would board a British Airlines plane that would take him first to London, where he would change planes for the final leg to Moscow. He used his last week in Delmarva to visit Svetlani at Hannah's as much as possible but there was never any time on her busy schedule for any kind of repeat of their Chincoteague adventure that neither would soon forget.

The time went by quickly and in about 24 hours, Bill would be on his way to Russia. He decided to drive to Dulles Airport in Washington and stay at the Marriott Hotel about 200 yards from the airport terminal. The Washington beltway traffic was notorious for backups and he didn't want to take any chance of missing his flight, and besides, staying at the hotel would enable him to get a good night of rest. The next morning, he didn't have to worry about setting his alarm because the jackhammers were already at work taking up the concrete on the old sidewalks right outside his bedroom window. As he boarded the plane that afternoon, his mind was still on Svetlani. He was worried she might think she was just a temporary fix until he could be with Olga but nothing was farther from the truth. He loved Svetlani as a dear friend and what was meant to be a day of leisure to relax and enjoy turned out to be much more when she spoke those few words that were still reverberating in his mind, "And Bill, if you get lonely tonight I will be here for you."

It was an act of love that neither had to be ashamed of because they cared a lot for each other. The leg to London was uneventful but he needed every moment to go through customs and security to get his connecting flight to Moscow. But now he was on his way and in less than three and a half hours, she would be waiting at the airport where four months earlier, over 40 people lost their lives and over two hundred more were injured when a suicide bomber decided innocent human beings have no value.

As he flew over Minsk, he thought about a girl by the name of Natalya he had met briefly at a popular breakfast place in Rehoboth this past year. She had lost one of her favorite customers when he succumbed in a car accident and every time Bill came in, she said he reminded her of Bob. She was now home in Belarus to visit her family. And like Natalya, her counterparts in Russia and the Ukraine, came to the USA to work long hours to earn enough money to go to school and help their families.

The British pilot announced that they would be landing at Domodedovo in 25 minutes, and now the exhilaration and anticipation of seeing Olga again was almost too overwhelming to contemplate. Finally, he was on the ground and he cleared security surprisingly quickly, as he picked up his luggage and headed toward the welcoming area, there she stood with her trademark smile. Olga epitomized the ultimate in womanhood because she had it all… grace, poise, charisma, sex appeal and most of all the ability to make you feel like you were the most important person on the planet. And now she was in his arms and he could not let her go or hold back the tears. They would be traveling companions for the next three weeks and that was all that mattered.

During the taxi ride from the airport to the Katerina Park Hotel, they discussed their itinerary. They would stay tonight in Moscow and in the morning a car dealership would deliver a sports car to the hotel that Olga's dad had purchased for her. Then after breakfast, they would drive to Kostroma, her home city, and that is where the trip would start. After their stay in Kostroma, they would embark on a 17 hour train ride to St. Petersburg and then take the Sapsan bullet train back to Moscow for the remainder of the time Bill would be in Russia. All this would be done in three weeks. Moscow would be busy for the next week because all the celebrations connected to the Great Patriotic War would be taking place and popular sites like Red Square would be cordoned off. When they arrived at the hotel, it was getting quite late because the traffic from the airport was very heavy. Their taxi driver, Voladna, was incredibly nice and extremely patient so Bill tipped him well. Voladna was from Kostroma and actually brought Olga from there to the airport, and it was his intention to make the five hour drive back this evening.

Olga and Bill had a sandwich and glass of Russian champagne at the hotel café before taking the elevator to the 8th floor where their rooms were right across from each other. The taste of the champagne was the same as Svetlani's mother had sent her from Russia. He remembered it had not only had a relaxing effect but put him in an amorous mood the night Svetlani invited him into her cabin at Chincoteague.

Now, as they got off the elevator, it was having a similar effect on him and he was hoping Olga would also get in the mood. He remembered while in the USA driving back home after dinner when Olga whispered, "Visit me in Russia and maybe something nice will happen." And of course, he interpreted that to mean they would be spending time in bed together so he suggested that they go to their separate rooms to freshen up and then he would come over to her room for a couple of hours before retiring for the night. "Bill, I would love to have you over but we are both exhausted. Since we have to get up early in the morning for the long drive to Kostroma, we need the rest. We will have other opportunities in the next three weeks."

Of course this made sense, since she had made the trip from Kostroma. They hugged and kissed and agreed to meet in the morning at 8am for breakfast. When Bill got in his room, he opened the window to allow the fresh air to enter since their centralized air conditioning system would not be turned on until the first of June. He slept soundly and when he met Olga at the breakfast buffet, she too looked rested and in high spirit giving Bill a warm hug and kiss. After breakfast, they went across the street to the park where veterans from the Great Patriotic War were running a mini-marathon.

Most were now in their late 80's and of course this was all part of the celebration to remember all those who sacrificed their lives in that war. It was an inspiring spectacle for sure and both of them cheered for every participant as they crossed the finish line. As they went back across the street, it was now 9 a.m. Representatives from the car dealership had just arrived with Olga's sports car and when they handed her the keys, she immediately christened it "my little baby."

On to Kostroma

They loaded their baggage in the back seat and now they were on their way to Kostroma. Bill had read so many stories about the historic town of Sergiev Posad so on the way they decided to stop there to view their majestic cathedral and grounds and the many shops that make and sell the famous Russian dolls. When they arrived there, a policeman flagged her down, noticing her temporary tags on her "little baby" and asked for paperwork regarding the transaction. Lucky for her, everything was in order and she could thank her dad, Andrey because he had made the purchase at the dealership. It was a common practice in Russia since terrorists use rental and recently purchased vehicles to do their evil deeds. Sergiev Posad is a place that Olga had never visited in all the years she lived in Russia and she thanked Bill for insisting to make it a part of their itinerary.

Now they were back on the road heading to Kostroma by way of Yaraslavi. The ride was a little scary with one lane of traffic in each direction, and with huge 18-wheelers coming toward you, passing slower cars was a real challenge. The displays of flowers along the roadside were testament to the legions of people who had lost their lives because someone had made the wrong decision. Olga had the courage, skill and common sense to deal with these conditions and her sport car had the "get up" when she called on it to make the pass. They were now approaching the industrial city of Yaraslavi when Olga decided to pull into McDonalds for some chicken nuggets and coke. Yes, American fast food outlets had become very popular in Russia, and in a way it was sad but modernity was taking place all across the globe and these types of stores were now becoming a part of their culture.

They were back on the road, and Kostroma was about 25 kilometers away when Olga stunned Bill. "Bill, since my return to Russia I have gotten re-acquainted with a wonderful guy, and we have a serious ongoing relationship and tomorrow, I will introduce him to you."

Wow!!! This was really big news but why didn't she mention him in all the letters she had sent to him?" Almost speechless, he could only respond by asking, "Has he brought happiness into your life, and what is his name?" "Yes, Bill, he has made me very happy and his name is Anthony."

Bill had a hundred questions to ask her but now was not a good time. It was only a short time before they would be arriving at the Azimuth Hotel where Bill would be staying for the next week. It was as if they had both lost their tongues because hardly a word was spoken between them until they arrived at the Azimuth parking lot. Olga seemed to be aware that he was miffed that she had not mentioned Anthony before he planned his trip here. She certainly had the right to enter into any relationship she desired but somehow the timing didn't seem appropriate. As Bill unloaded his travel bag, they gave each other a tepid hug and kiss with her informing him that she would be here tomorrow to pick him up for some sightseeing at 10am. Since this was Olga's hometown, she would be staying at her own rental flat.

When he got settled into his very comfortable room, all the questions he wanted to ask her entered his mind. Just last night at the Katerina Park Hotel in Moscow when Bill wanted to spend a few hours with her in her room she promised "There will be other opportunities in the next three weeks." Being able to share a bed with her was an important part of coming here, although seeing this giant piece of the planet was always something he wanted to do. The questions kept popping into his head.

How much did she tell Anthony about him? Did she tell him of their near-death experience during the day of the 100 year storm in Chincoteague? How about their night at the Quality Inn? Was he also from Kostroma and was he aware that she would be traveling with him to St. Petersburg and Moscow? Did they intend to have a monogamous relationship or a more liberal one? Eventually, all these questions would need to be answered, but now it was time to go to sleep because tomorrow would be a busy day.

When Bill awoke the next morning, he took his shower, had the breakfast buffet, and walked around the grounds of the hotel and waited for Olga to get there with her "little baby." (aka: her sport car). When she arrived 30 minutes later than the time they agreed to meet, he pretended not to notice her tardiness or anything that had transpired the night before regarding the revelation that Anthony was a very important part of her life. So he gave her a very friendly upbeat greeting, "Good morning most beautiful lady in the universe." This brought a big smile to her face and she seemed to recognize that if he was hurt, he was being a good sport and would be able to accept Anthony as a friend.

But now was the time to see Kostroma and visit as many of the places and sites he had read about in this historic city. As they drove toward the bridge that would take them across the Volga River, she decided the best place to start their day would be Susanikaya Square which is considered the heart of the city. The architecture was a good example of the 18th century opulence that was prevalent at the time. The Palace of General Borsht and the Ipatiev Monastery were good examples. It was at the latter that Mikhail Romanoff was appointed the first Tsar of Russia in 1613 by the ruling committee in Moscow. Although only 16 at the time, he accepted the challenge and ruled for a period of several decades. There was a statue of Susanin on top of the hill that led to the Volga River. Legend has it that a peasant by the name of Susanin led the invading Polish Army into the swamps, where they all perished including himself. There are other versions of this story but nonetheless to the people of Kostroma, both past and present, he was their hero. Of course, in the park behind the Square, there is a statue of Lenin, hand extended as if he were saying, "Follow me."

As they sat on the bench at the picturesque water fountain, Olga told the story of the time she came here as a four year old on a hot July day; removing all her clothes and standing under the cooling water to escape the heat of the day. Her mother dealt with her boldness with a few well-placed spanks on the butt. Perhaps, her early effrontery was a sign of what the future would hold for her. But now was the time to pick up Anthony at his place of work. He would meet the man who Olga confessed had brought so much happiness into her life. He was hoping he could keep his jealousy in check because despite the disparity in age between him and Olga, he was so smitten by her, he could not stand the thought that someone else would be sharing her bed and benefitting from her warm embraces.

And as Anthony walked out of his work place toward her "little baby," he was impressive from the start, with a calm demeanor and engaging personality. Almost immediately, Bill understood why Olga could be attracted to him. With good looks and poise, he also had a great sense of humor when he posed this question, "Bill, why are you trying to steal my Olga?"

It was delivered in such a way that they all got a big chuckle as they entered the rear grounds of the Ipatiev Monastery to have lunch at the church café. Bill had noticed on the ride over that Anthony who was now driving her "little baby" would move his right hand to her inner thigh and do a little rub as if he were saying, "This lady belongs to me." Although Bill had gained great respect for Anthony, he was finding it difficult to suppress his jealousy and wondered if he could contain it throughout his stay in Kostroma. The lunch at the café was very special and as they pondered the grounds with its brooks and ponds, Bill could not help to wonder if the gardens were here when Tsar Mikhail I resided there in 1613.

"Ladies of the Night"

The lunch of cabbage soup and dacha dumplings was delightful, but the only downside was there was only one beautiful woman, and she belonged to Anthony. Now, Bill had serious doubts whether he would be sharing the bed with her for even a minute during his entire stay in Russia. During their walk on these hallowed grounds, they had built five log houses to give visitors a taste of what 18th century living was all about both in the city and villages surrounding areas like Kostroma and Yaraslavi.

The day was getting late and it was now time to go over to the Kostroma Train Depot to purchase two tickets for Olga and Bill for their 17 hour train ride to St. Petersburg later in the week.

He was also anxious to see the little café located there that he read about where someone had written a review of how tasty and cheap the food was and how it was prepared from scratch in about 10 minutes for about 90 rubles. When he peeked in, he got a surprise when two "ladies of the night" darted toward him, no doubt eyeing him as a potential customer. As they got closer, they lifted up their skirts to where their underpants were showing. Olga grabbed Bill from the back of his shirt and pulled him away, admonishing him at the same time that this was precisely what she was trying to protect him from while visiting her country.

After obtaining their train tickets, the three of them drove away toward Bill's hotel where they left him off. When he got into the lobby, he asked the desk clerk to call a cab because he wanted to visit the two ladies at the café. It wasn't sex Bill was looking for, but instead he wanted to interview them to get a first-hand glimpse of why two pretty ladies chose to enter into the dark world of prostitution.

When he arrived back at the train depot and entered the café, they were still there and in a blink of the eye, they were off their chairs offering him a two for one deal. Bill was surprised that their English was proficient enough that there would be no misunderstandings about price or expectations. For 5000 rubles, they would be at his service for one hour. He agreed that their offer was more than fair, but when he explained that he wasn't there for sex, but just wanted a one hour interview regarding their lives as "ladies of the night." They looked at each other as if they didn't understand. But after some more explaining they seemed to grasp his intent and probably thought he was a little weird. They had a two bedroom flat across the street from the depot and there is where the interview would take place. Because there was a steady flow of police vehicles in the area, he had no fear for his safety. As an added precaution, Bill showed them his wallet that contained one thousand rubles… enough for his taxi fare to his hotel. The Depot had several ATM's and he would extract 2500 rubles now and after the interview, they would come back to the Depot to extract the remaining 2500 rubles. They seemed to sense that he was honest and they agreed to the arrangement. As they walked across the street, he finally got around to asking them their names and they gave Luba and Kira. When they opened the door to enter their flat, Bill was surprised how clean and tidy everything was. They presented him with a short tour of their unit and he took notice that their bedrooms were arranged in such a way to put any man in the mood very quickly. The colors were very pleasing to the eye and the sheets and bedding were immaculate.

He would not be conducting any business in the bedrooms, but instead their kitchen and small table would suffice. Bill led off with questions about their families… parents, children, husbands or ex-husbands, and even their boyfriends and they both seemed eager to talk about it all. They were divorced with two children each, all living with mothers or grandparents. Neither chose prostitution, but it was the quickest way to obtain the money required to meet their obligations.

The winters were harsh in Russia and this way, they could afford to buy adequate clothing and footwear for their children. Both Luba and Kira had part time jobs in a shoe factory outside Kostroma so prostitution was not their only income. As far as their children and parents knew, the factory is where they derived all their income and the families had no idea that they were also working as "ladies of the night." Also, by working at the shoe factory, they were able to obtain all the shoes for their families at the production cost which was a huge savings. Their ex-husbands were working in the energy business somewhere in Siberia, and now and then they would send a few rubles to help out, but it was all too infrequent.

Bill was careful not to ask any political questions because just like in the USA, it was too hot to handle and usually ended badly. The hour was about over and he was impressed that both Kira and Luba wanted to tell their story and they sensed in Bill that he was sympathetic with their plight. In fact, Luba confessed that she had become very fond of Bill and wanted to demonstrate in some small way her feelings for him.

She knelt on her knees and touched him on his most sensitive part, trying to unbuckle his belt at the same time. Bill intervened by picking her up and reminding her a deal is a deal and oral sex was not a part of it. She could not believe that he had the will power to resist her advance. He then reminded them it was time to cross the street and get their remaining 2500 rubles. He gave each a heartfelt hug and kiss. Instead of taking out the 2500 rubles, he took out the maximum the machine allowed which was 7500 rubles. He requested that they use the extra 5000 rubles to purchase something nice for their children. He understood that they knew best what their most pressing needs were and whatever they decided was okay with him. They walked him to his taxi and they embraced each other as if they were old friends.

On his ride back to the hotel, Bill began to think that Russia and its people were just as beautiful as all their magnificent palaces and cathedrals. He never asked them their ages but somewhere between 30 and 35 would be a good guess. He was happy he was able to see the other side of Russian society, where love of family was so important to them that they were willing to sacrifice their bodies and self-esteem to be sure those that depended on them could purchase at least the bare essentials if nothing more. He didn't know whether he would ever see Kira and Luba again, but he would never forget them. To him, they were special because they cared so much for those they loved. Olga had warned him to stay away from the seedy side of Russia but had he listened, he would have missed the human side that was so real and poignant. In fact, now that Anthony had become such a big part of Olga's life, he now had the freedom to meet and maybe even begin a new relationship with someone else.

The morning had arrived quickly and Olga and Anthony would be here shortly for their day trip to Plyos. This time, they were both on time, and Bill was hoping he would not slip and tell them where he had gone after they left him off last night. Olga had a Russian temper and she would not tolerate conduct she deemed inappropriate. But now they were approaching Plyos. The view from the hillside above the town is truly a majestic panorama, unrivaled for its scenic beauty, where the mighty Volga cuts off the main town from the Russian forest on the other side. No wonder they called this gem the "Russian Switzerland." Just using his imagination, he could think what it might look like in December after a nice snowfall. It would truly be a winter wonderland. In its infancy, it was a town of wooden houses and buildings and had been burnt to the ground on many occasions by rival factions understanding its strategic value as a port on the Volga. Now it is a very important destination for the tourist river cruises in what is known as "The Golden Ring," which includes towns and cities along the Volga such as Kostroma and Yaraslavi. The 3000 residents operate small souvenir and fish kiosks to service the visitors along its main street. What is so nice is that many of the souvenirs are handmade bracelets, pencils, etc. from their native wood which is what most people prefer, rather than cheap jewelry that is probably made in some Asian factory. Its quaint café offers a good variety of native fare always starting with their cabbage soups and dishes. Plyos is and was a favorite place to visit for the rich and famous, such as English royalty and wealthy European businessmen looking for a private getaway.

Their day at Plyos was ending, and it was a hard place to leave. Bill vowed to return one day to lease or rent one of the dachas sprinkled along the hillsides. It was now time for the short ride back to Kostroma and tomorrow would be "Olga Day," so designated to honor the life of Olga Kornakova. Bill wanted a special day for her and seeing where she went to school, her church, her swimming, dancing, and exercise facilities were all very important for him and after visiting all these venues, they would go to her parent's home for a Russian feast. It was a day he would not have to share with Anthony until dinner time.

"Olga Day," and Dinner with Marina and Andrey

When they went by the early grade school that Olga attended, it was recess time and Bill imagined that one of those pretty girls on the playground was her. She even pointed out some of the secret places where she would meet some of her early boyfriends in her formative teenage years. Bill's imagination was now at lightning speed, wishing he could have been with her in those times. There was little doubt that Russian life was flowing through his veins because today's Russia was similar to the years he grew up in the USA many decades earlier.

It was now getting close to the time they would be going to her parent's home and Bill insisted on stopping at the spirit store and florist to purchase a bottle of vodka for Andrey and some roses for Marina. His day with Olga alone was about to end because now it was time to go by Anthony's workplace to pick him up for their feast engagement at the Kornakova's. When they entered the very comfortable apartment, they removed their shoes and the aroma of the main dish now cooking in the oven was a reminder that this Russian dinner was going to be something very special. Bill had seen pictures of Marina. Her beauty was obvious, but meeting her in person, her warmth and kindness were the personification of beauty in its purest form. She was so gracious, and made you feel like you were part of the family from the very start. Olga's dad, Andrey, reminded him of the "Rock of Gibraltar." Strong, rugged and handsome and someone you didn't want to mess with. Now Bill knew why Olga reminded him of the Goddess of Love because having such outstanding parents with their obvious physical assets, she had to be uniquely beautiful. Marina treated Bill to a couple of picture albums showing their lives together as Olga matured into this lady he loved so much. The pork roast in the oven had been rubbed down with some mixture of spices that had been handed down from one generation to another since the days of the Tsars.

Marina requested Bill to assist her in removing the roaster pan from the oven, which by tradition was an honor bestowed on a special guest. When he removed the lid, the sight of the roast surrounded by the carrots, potatoes and turnips in the savory juice reminded him of the times as a young boy, helping his mom in removing their pot roast from their coal-fired oven. Now it was time to take the family butcher knife and slice this heavenly piece of pig. Needless to say, this meal was fit for a king and maybe even a Tsar like Peter the Great.

When the evening ended, Bill realized his life had been enriched immeasurably because Marina and Andrey had impressed him even beyond his lofty expectations. The time had passed so quickly while in the Kostroma Oblast and tomorrow evening, he and Olga would board a train for their 17 hour ride to St. Petersburg. He was going to miss Kostroma and all the friendly people he had met, including stalwarts in the community like Marina, Andrey and Anthony, but also those who were struggling to meet their everyday needs like Luba and Kira.

The next day had come quickly and it was going to be a spectacular day. They would be leaving for St. Petersburg this evening but until then, they decided to drive out to the Romanoff Forest for a day of leisure and relaxation. And what a place it was with all the grandeur in the days of the Tsars but yet the quiet serenity of its deep forests just a few kilometers from the opulent hotel and restaurants sharing this same piece of the planet. The three of them had a nice lunch on the veranda of one of the Cafés and Bill remembered he had seen this same venue in a picture Olga had sent to him.

She was standing there in her winter coat after a heavy snowfall had blanketed the area, and he always wondered who took that picture of her. Now he knew it was Anthony. It was now May and the picture had been taken at least a few months earlier and at that time, Bill didn't have a clue there was an Anthony in her life. Nevertheless, even if he had known about Anthony, he would have still come to Russia because that was his boyhood dream, and he was grateful to Olga for inviting him and making his dream come true. Without a doubt, this part of the Romanoff Forest was exquisite in both design and elegance, and the food was delicious. Bill actually wrote a note in the chef's diary congratulating him on the quality of his offerings.

But now it was time to drive back to Kostroma, because in less than five hours, they would be on the train and Bill wanted to give Anthony and Olga a few hours to be with each other, as it would be at least two weeks before she would return to Kostroma. They left Bill off at his hotel to pack and take care of his hotel bill as well as taking a final hot shower. They would return at 6pm for the ride to the depot. When they arrived there they were already boarding passengers and it was time to shake hands with Anthony and thank him for allowing Olga to be with him. Of course, she's a very independent woman and Anthony probably understood she was going to do whatever she wished.

The Seventeen Hour Train Ride

When Bill got on the steps of the train, he looked back at the depot with fond memories because there is where he met Luba and Kira. After boarding, Bill and Olga went to their assigned four person cabin where he claimed the left side lower bed and she chose the upper bed above him. Soon, a sprightly English lady arrived by the name of Parker Standish arrived and she would take the remaining lower bed or bunk. Now they would wait to see who would come to claim the last upper berth.

Parker Standish showed no shyness when she learned that Bill was from the USA, immediately letting him know she was a descendant of Miles (Myles) Standish. Bill, being well versed in early American history, remembered him as the head person and leader on the ship The Mayflower which carried a group of disgruntled English citizens to America in the late 17th century, and they would form an enclave to be known as The Pilgrim Colony. It was in the part of the country now known as Massachusetts. Supposedly they left England to escape religious persecution. Nonetheless, her name was Standish and she was from England and there was no reason for him to challenge her claim. As the train began to pull away, the person who was to claim the last berth in their cabin arrived and introduced himself as Mikhail Popovich. He was Russian but spoke fluent English which made it easier for the four of them to have conversations of mutual interest. After introducing himself, he gave everyone a wooden medallion with the Russian bear emblazoned on one side and the Ipatiev Monastery on the flip side as a gesture of friendship.

Later, when the train stopped in the town of Nerehta to pick up passengers and add two more cars, Bill and Olga went to the convenience store to buy some cookies. When they resumed their journey, they were able to share their goodies with Mikhail and Ms. Standish. The train steward motioned for Olga to come to the preparation area where she had brewed some hot tea. Olga was given the chore of taking the tea to their cabin. They sat around the two lower bunks to chat while enjoying their refreshments.

Mikhail's Demise

It was about 10pm when Mikhail decided to retire for the evening, pulling himself to the upper berth above Parker Standish. He too showed no sign of shyness by choosing to sleep in the nude. You could hardly blame him for wanting to do so because the upper berths were very warm. In fact, the entire cabin was overly warm so Bill decided to remove his jeans and sleep in his underwear but when Parker Standish objected, he had no choice but to keep his pants on. Olga came to Bill's defense by telling Ms. Standish it was no big deal to see a man in his underwear and for her to be skittish was a bit silly. Parker countered by challenging Olga to sleep in her underwear since what is good for the goose is good for the gander. Olga didn't seem to have a good response for this counter-attack but Bill, sensing an altercation was possible, decided to diffuse the matter by saying he would just unbuckle his belt and upper button and at least it would make him feel cooler. But he added, "Olga, if you decide to sleep in your panties and bra or nothing at all, I have no objections." By this time, Mikhail was sound asleep and his breathing sounded heavy.

When Bill awoke about 5am the two ladies were sound asleep and Mikhail had put on his trousers and shirt and collected his travel bag, slipping Bill a note, whispering very softly not to open it until he was alone. He gave Bill a friendly wave goodbye and never returned to their cabin. Bill noticed that he looked pale and his breathing was heavy.

Bill put the note in the secret compartment of his belt and would wait until he got to his room in St. Petersburg before opening it. By this time the ladies were still sound asleep and since it would be only a few hours before getting to St. Petersburg he decided to take his little souvenir whistle and awake them from their slumber. Later as the train pulled into the station, Parker asked Bill why Mikhail never returned to the cabin to at least say goodbye. He was an extremely friendly man and a real gentleman and it did seem very unusual. Bill kept his thoughts to himself, thinking that maybe it had something to do with the note he had been given by Mikhail. As Bill and Olga walked to get a taxi, they bid a fond farewell to Parker Standish. Although they both thought she was a little prudish, in reality she was a real nice lady. On the taxi ride over to the hotel naturally Bill did not disclose to Olga anything that had transpired between him and Mikhail except to say he whispered goodbye and God bless, giving a wave of the hand as he departed the cabin. They were enjoying the sounds and sights of this magnificent city and when their taxi pulled up to the front entrance of the Azimut Hotel, they both expressed how surprisingly good they felt after their 17 hour journey.

So, when they got into the lobby, they decided to sign up for the midnight to 3am mini-tour of the city. Since they would only be here for a week, they wanted to be sure to take advantage of every hour they spent here. There was so much to see and do in this history rich city and they both understood they would not be getting their usual amount of sleep while here. It was now two in the afternoon and Olga wanted to go to her room for a warm shower and then do a little window shopping in the stores around and in the vicinity of the hotel.

They agreed to meet in the lobby at 11pm this evening to have a drink before their midnight tour just in case they didn't see each other sooner. So this would give plenty of time to go to his room and open the note Mikhail had given to him. Since his writing was very legible, he had no problem reading its contents and his words shook Bill so much he had to lay down because it about took his breath away.

"Mr. Bill, be very careful of this lady Olga. I taught a class when I was in the Russian Intelligence Service and she was one of my students. Our agency recruited and trained young girls of high intellect and great beauty on how to use their assets to attract men in the USA and the West and use them as covers in their spying activities. Don't worry about her recognizing me because in those days I was heavily disguised. Good luck and God bless, Mikhail."

Wow!!! To say Bill felt betrayed would not adequately describe his feelings. This woman he cared so much about was now someone he had to fear. He had used self-hypnosis to convince himself she was not a spy and now this. He thought they had a special bond after their near-death experience at Chincoteague. He came to Russia to be with her and on occasion to share a bed with her and then discovered there was an Anthony in her life. But this was the time to stay cool and calm and be alert. He decided to try to take a short nap because at 11pm he would be meeting with her and wanted to be rested.

When he awoke it was now 9pm and he decided to go to the bar in the lobby for a drink to calm his nerves. He was still in a state of disbelief after reading Mikhail's note and he would have to find a way to be as normal as possible when she arrived.

The Russian bartender, Vladimir, was very friendly and since he was not busy, he engaged Bill in conversation. When he learned that he was from the USA, he began to ask him questions about what parts of Russia he had visited. Bill related to him that he had spent a week in the Kostroma Oblast and had just arrived this morning on the overnight train.

"That must have been the train where a man fell on the tracks about 200 kilometers east of here." Bill could not believe his ears since he had not heard of the incident while on the train. "Was the man identified?"

"Yes, his name was Mikhail, which is the same name as my father-in-law who just happens to work for the railroad, and he was the one who told me of the unfortunate incident." Bill was stunned and wondered if this could be the same Mikhail who shared their cabin and if so what were the circumstances surrounding the incident. Did he end his own life or did he just fall? He was hoping it was not the Mikhail who had given him the note but regardless, it was a precious life and someone's loved one had perished.

It was now approaching 11pm and Olga would be here soon and he decided not to tell her what Vladimir had told him although she had probably already learned of the incident through her RIS contacts. The story would be in the morning papers and he would wait until then to learn more. But now Olga had arrived and after having a glass of wine and discussing her day of shopping they boarded the tour bus. A lady who introduced herself as Nina would be their guide. Since Bill was the only non-Russian on the bus, she gave him special attention and during their various stops, Bill would ask Olga to take a picture of him and Nina with one of the attractions behind them such as the Trinity Cathedral or a statue of Peter the Great on his horse. On several occasions, he would ask Nina if he could put his arms around her on these photo-ops, which she was happy to oblige. Although Olga gave the impression that she was not jealous it was apparent she was by holding his hand on subsequent stops. One of the highlights of the tour was to watch all the draw bridges open on the Neva River at exactly 1:25am. There was little doubt that their stay in this city of a thousand attractions would be exciting and exhilarating and tonight would be a great start.

By the time they got back to their hotel it was already 3am and now reality had set in and Olga decided to go to her room to get some sleep. Bill opted to stick around in the lobby until the morning papers arrived. He must have dozed off because when he opened his eyes, the big clock above the revolving doors read 5:30am and by this time, the morning papers should be arriving so he went over to the desk clerk and she just happened to be reading the St. Petersburg Times.

Bill excused himself for interrupting but asked if that was this morning's edition and she said yes. Since she wasn't busy, he explained to her that he was trying to get information about the train accident yesterday where a man lost his life. She was kind enough to peruse each page, and sure enough, on page five, she found the article and began to read it to him. His name was Mikhail Popovich, age 60, and police requested the railroad to release the names of three passengers who shared the cabin with him where all had boarded in Kostroma. The article went on to list the names and they were; Parker Standish holding a British passport, Bill Bond from the USA and Olga Kornakova of the Russian Federation.

They were to report to the authorities in St. Petersburg within three days. Bill thanked her and now so shaken he sat down on one of the lounge chairs in the lobby to try to absorb it all. He was sure Olga was involved up to her eyeballs. The implications were enormous and instinctively he understood he had to make a decision on what to do with the note Mikhail had given to him.

He had not slept except for short naps and they were scheduled to go to Peterhof at 10am and regardless of what was going on all around him, it was one attraction he didn't want to miss. He had just enough time to take his morning shower and have a couple pastries before she would be here. He kept the note in his belt before departing for their tour, suspecting that RIS agents would be searching his room not long after getting on the bus. When she arrived, she noticed that he was not eating a hearty breakfast and asked if he was feeling okay. He attributed his lack of appetite to staying up late the night before and since he had read there was a nice lunch place on the site, he could wait to reinforce his energy level.

When they arrived at Peterhof there were not adequate adjectives to describe its opulence and splendor. Peter the Great had travelled to Versailles, near Paris to get some ideas for his masterpiece but many believe it surpasses Versailles in all levels of artistic grandeur. The Grand Palace and its grounds were now commercialized with vendors, but as they removed their shoes and put on the slippers provided, none of that mattered because as they went from room to room in this wondrous Palace one was awe stricken with its history.

Bill Meets Dasha Brumel

Catherine the Great would spend many weeks here to be with her various lovers and as you walked through her bedroom suite you could only imagine what went on here. Later, strolling the grounds with its fountains and bronze and marble statues it felt as if you were in another era and you were proud and happy that you could be in the past with them if only for a fleeting moment.

Before getting on the bus and heading back to St. Petersburg they went over to the lunch pavilion to have some Russian pancakes and hot chocolate. Olga had thus far failed to mention the demise of Mikhail and their obligation to report to the authorities sometime in the next few days. He began to wonder whether Parker Standish had gotten the word and how she would react. She was a very feisty and independent woman and he was sure she would not look kindly on their request to appear since she talked about being on a very tight schedule. Of course, that was her concern and Bill had enough on his plate without being too concerned about someone quite capable of taking care of herself.

When they arrived back at the hotel, Olga finally broke her silence by letting Bill know that she had called the RIS headquarters in St. Petersburg and arranged for a 3pm meeting tomorrow for both of them. She went on to explain that although they would go together, they would be interviewed separately in different rooms within the facility by different interrogators. She continued by saying that he would be getting special treatment because the chief interrogator from the Moscow office would be taking the Sapsan bullet train up in the morning and she would interview Bill.

Wow!! A woman would be interviewing him and already he began to suspect that she would be using tactics that Mikhail had warned him about in the note. The fact that the RIS were involved instead of local police authorities was making him feel very uncomfortable and he knew it was now time to dispose of the note Mikhail had given him. He visited the public bathroom in the hotel, took the note from his belt, tore it into a hundred pieces and flushed it down the toilet. It was now late so he went to his room to lie down. Olga, the woman he came over to be with was in a room just two doors down from him. It was almost surreal because now there was no chance that he would be sharing a bed with her as he had hoped and envisioned when he was in Delmarva. In fact, he wondered if he could even get it up if she invited him over and stripped down to nothing laying there with her beguiling smile motioning with her index finger to join her.

With all those thoughts running through his mind, he wasn't sure what time he fell asleep but when he awoke the next morning, it was already 10am. All he could think about was the 3pm appointment he had at RIS headquarters. By the time he had his breakfast and took his morning walk, it was noon and he had not yet seen Olga. To pass the time away and calm his nerves, he sat down and began to read a book he had purchased at Peterhof telling how Peter the Great's daughter the Empress Elizabeth and Catherine the Great had taken his ideas he didn't have time to implement before his death and acted upon them to enhance and add to its magnificence and make it into what it is today.

When he had gotten about half way through this compelling read, Olga tapped him on the shoulder from behind and said their taxi was waiting to take them for their interviews. When they arrived at the RIS offices, Olga was whisked away to some location on the premises that was obviously pre-arranged. Of course, she had informed him yesterday that they would be interviewed separately, so this was no surprise. As he sat there on a bench near the entry door, a friendly diminutive man approached and introduced himself as Yuri and asked Bill to follow him. They entered a room that looked nothing like the one he had imagined, thinking it would be a dark and foreboding location as he had seen in movies back in the 40's depicting Soviet style interrogation methods. The room was well lit with soft lights and a giant skylight that was allowing the southwest sun to enter. There was an indoor garden where orchids and roses were the dominant theme.

There were two comfortable lounge chairs with leg rests facing each other about four meters apart and Yuri pointed to the one he wanted Bill to take, with "Make yourself comfortable, Ms. Brumel will be with you shortly." Soon, she appeared and there was little doubt she was Russian, whom he always thought were among the most beautiful and glamorous women on the planet. And if there was a lady who could compete with Olga for pure natural beauty she was a worthy contender. Her natural full lips would put Delilah to shame and her smile so seductive a man could be ready in minutes if the opportunity afforded itself. She wore a one piece sky blue dress and with her breasts showing just a centimeter away from her nipples which could be noticed through her thin cotton dress. As she sat down in the chair facing him, she made good use of her leg rests and her legs were so lovely and when she moved them just slightly her white underpants would show. The circulation of blood in his body was now affecting his most sensitive body part and he was wondering if she had noticed. She flashed another seductive smile and then she introduced herself. "Good afternoon Mr. Bond, my name is Dasha Brumel and I will be conducting this interview on behalf of my office within the RIS. I trust your visit to Russia has been a pleasant one so far and I promise I will not keep you any longer than necessary, I know you want to get on with your vacation and we are extremely proud of St. Petersburg and its rich history and when you leave Russia I am quite sure you will feel that your life has been enriched. There is ice water and tea on the stand to the right so feel free to have a sip of either if you feel thirsty."

"I will be recording our dialogue with this device and you will be given a transcript of all that is discussed… are you ready?" Bill nodded his head to say he was ready.

"Can you give me a brief description of Mikhail when you first met him, in other words what was your initial impression of him?"

"He was a very nice man with a great sense of humor and a personality that made you feel at ease very quickly."

"I see when he learned you were from the USA, how did he greet you?

"He shook my hand and gave me a wooden medallion with the Russian bear stamped on one side and the Ipatiev Monastery on the other which I considered it to be a special gesture of friendship."

"Yes, of course I understand do you have the medallion with you and if so, can I take a look at it?"

"Yes, I have it here in my pocket and I would be most happy to show it to you."

"I have seen them at various souvenir shops as I travel around Russia, almost always having the Russian bear on the front side with some landmark of the particular Oblast they are being sold from on the reverse side. Thank you for allowing me to see it. Did you observe anything unusual about him or his actions during your trip?"

"No, except he chose to sleep in the nude which seemed to be a little odd but I can't say I blame him since it was very warm in the two upper berths."

"It is not so odd here in Russia and you may have noticed that the ladies are not afraid to show off their sexuality. Anyway, how did Parker Standish and Olga react when they observed his immodesty?"

"I hope you don't mind if I throw in a little humor here but Ms. Standish never saw him since he was in the bunk above her but when I wanted to sleep in my underwear because the entire cabin was uncomfortably warm, she objected and Olga chided her asking what was so unusual about seeing a man in his underwear. Can I continue?"

"Yes of course go ahead and finish it is getting interesting."

"Then a small altercation got underway when Parker asked Olga why she didn't strip down to her panties and bra because after all what is so unusual about seeing a woman in her underwear."

"That is all very funny, anyway how did it all end?"

"I could see the situation was getting out of hand so I intervened by offering a compromise, promising to just loosen my belt and open the tops of my pants so at least I would feel a little cooler. Poor Mikhail was sleeping soundly through all this and that seemed to diffuse the matter and in a few minutes everything was back to normal"

"Oh, those English ladies are so proper aren't they? And by the way, did Olga decide to sleep in her underwear?"

"No such luck."

"I have a few more questions for you and then we can wrap it up. Did Mikhail give you anything else besides the wooden medallion?"

"Yes, he handed me a note before departing the cabin wishing me a wonderful visit to St. Petersburg and then good luck and God bless, Mikhail."

"I wonder why he wrote you a note instead of just verbally expressing his thoughts and wishes."

"There were several reasons why he may have done it this way but his main reason in my opinion was that he knew I kept a book with people's well wishes either written in it, or if they just handed me a note or autograph I would tape them in carefully. Sadly I had left this book in my main luggage which I had shipped earlier to my hotel in St. Petersburg. I made a mistake by just putting it in my pocket where I also keep my rubles for taxi fares."

"Do you have the note with you and if so can I have a look at it?"

"No, that is why I told you I made a mistake when I put it in my pocket where I kept my rubles and when I got out of the taxi near the canal downtown, the rubles and note were together when a sudden rush of wind blew both the rubles and note into the canal. The rubles could be replaced but not the note and it made me very sad."

"Do you think you could identify the driver if you saw him or her again?"

"Yes, I remember him very well and when he saw what happened, he seemed to sense my loss. I had additional rubles in my wallet to pay him but the note was important to me."

EDITORS NOTE: At this point it is important to explain why Bill told Dasha Brumel about a note handed to him by Mikhail Popovich just in case Olga had one eye open when he departed the train. The actual note that he gave Bill warning him of Olga's connection to the

Russian Intelligence Service was torn into a hundred pieces and flushed down the public toilet at the Azimuth Hotel. Also, Bill actually had rubles blown out of his hand near the Canal and thinking that it might help him when being questioned, made a point of his loss to the taxi driver.

Dasha Brumel continued her questioning.

"Did Mikhail tell you where he was going when he departed your cabin?"

"No, leaving the cabin that early made little sense to me at the time but I remember his heavy breathing and that his face was pale so now in retrospect, I understand he was looking for a place to get some fresh air."

"Did he tell you why he was visiting St. Petersburg?"

"Yes, the evening before while sitting around having our cookies and tea, he explained he was going to visit his sister whom he hadn't seen in over a decade. I don't remember if he mentioned her name or what part of St. Petersburg she lived in."

"When and where did you meet Olga Kornakova?"

"I met her this summer at a very popular dining place on the water in Delmarva called Hannah's."

"Did she work there?"

"Yes, it was a very hot and sultry evening and I will never forget it. I was dining with my very good friends Dr. Bob Moser and his most beautiful wife Suzanne and their two children Soren and Maggie. I always do a little flirting with the ladies and I can't remember what line I used that evening but our friendship clicked from the very start."

"Was Olga the reason you decided to visit Russia?"

"I always wanted to visit Russia since the 4th grade when I observed on the maps we studied the vastness of this giant country. Of course, those were the Soviet days and we were allies in the Great Patriotic War or what we called World War 2. After that the cold war began between our two countries and any chance to obtain the necessary visas to enter Russia was nearly impossible. But yes, when Olga invited me to visit her in Russia, I was ecstatic because after all those years wishing to go there she gave me the opportunity and probably without her encouragement I would not be here."

"Don't worry, I won't ask you any personal questions about your relationship with her or maybe I should say your friendship with her."

"Thank you I appreciate that."

"Well, Mr. Bond, I hope I haven't inconvenienced you too much. I believe you came here with Olga and she will be waiting for you in the lobby. I will have Yuri take both of you to your hotel in our official car. I will be riding with you since he will continue on from there to the train depot where I will take the 6pm Sapsan back to Moscow. Here is my card and if you can think of anything else that might help us with our investigation into Mikhail's unfortunate death, please get in touch with me."

"I will and thanks for treating me so well."

A Taste of Olga's Anger

The ride back to the hotel was quite revealing. Olga and Dasha pretended not to know each other well but Bill was alert to notice that if indeed they were colleagues in the RIS their relationship was strained. They were both spectacularly beautiful women but it was easy to see there was a little intramural competition between them. Bill had read that the Russian Intelligence Service was very compartmentalized with a domestic and international branch and because of the great importance both put on secretiveness, many times one didn't know what the other was up to.

This happens in the USA with our CIA, FBI, and the NSA. Olga was no doubt in the international branch and Dasha the domestic branch. Since this incident happened within the jurisdiction of Ms. Brumel, the investigation was under her purview. They were both about the same age so whether one outranked the other, it didn't matter and of course at this time Olga had no idea that Bill was aware she had RIS connections. Dasha put her scent mark down by asking Olga to sit up front with Yuri while she shared the back seat with Bill. For sure, Olga was noticing that Dasha had now pulled her dress up and her panties were showing giving him a good view of her picture- perfect legs and then some. Bill was both amused and flattered that these two exceptional women were vying for his attention and when Dasha moved her leg against his and was actually touching his knee with her hand.

Olga was furious and although she didn't mutter a word her face had turned a jealous red and there would be hell to pay later when they got to the hotel. Olga tried to hide her anger by reminding everyone that she and Bill would be going to dinner tonight at the famous Stroganoff

Steak House and then on to the theater to see the ballet. It was Olga's way of saying that you are having your fun now but he will be with me and I will be receiving the benefits of his company at both venues and maybe I will give him the entire package after these engagements, not just some cheap tease.

When they arrived at the hotel Yuri opened the door for Olga while Dasha was saying goodbye to Bill, ending by giving him a tight hug and meaningful kiss. He remembered from Mikhail's note that female operatives were expected to use their assets to gain favor and this was no doubt a demonstration of that early training but also an attempt to make Olga jealous. She again reminded Bill to call her in Moscow if he remembered anything about Mikhail that they had not covered in the interview. Of course all Bond men interpret these invitations to call as perhaps an opportunity to meet the person in some private setting and since he would be in Moscow in a few days maybe that was her intent. But Olga was not in a good mood as they walked into the lobby of the Azimut and it didn't take long to vent her anger with these remarks, "For her to dress like that rubbing her leg against yours and displaying practically all her breasts was shameful. And you sitting there no doubt with a hard-on made no effort to move away."

"I guess you were hoping she would move her hand from your knee to your dick. And Yuri with his eye on the rear view mirror instead of the road with a smile on his face was also disgusting behavior. There is something about that woman I don't like or trust and she would probably go to bed with any Tom, Dick, or Harry and especially Dick."

Wow!!! That was quite a statement to make considering their positions in the same organization. Bill then asked her if their dinner and theater engagement was still on for this evening and she continued with this, "Yes, but I hope you will show me some respect by not fixating your eyes on every set of breasts like some immature schoolboy." With that, she scurried to her room to probably vent her anger in some private way with her sometimes very spirited language. Later, when she appeared in the lobby for their evening engagement, Bill could not believe the outfit she had chosen. No woman had more natural beauty than Olga, and she decided to enhance her assets by wearing a leopard skin mini-skirt and a matching low cut blouse featuring two snarling leopards with their teeth strategically placed in the middle of her two voluptuous breasts.

No Greek Goddess or Risulki Temptress could have possibly been more seductive than her. Bill understood that he was extremely fortunate to have her as his dinner partner but at the same time, he could not remove from his mind that she was involved with the demise of Mikhail. If she invited him to her room later tonight, what should he do? If he refused, she would wonder how he could possibly turn her down and would be suspicious that he had learned that she was an RIS operative and therefore tied in some way to Mikhail.

He could always say he had so much respect for Anthony and considered him a valued friend and valued friends don't fuck their friend's wives or girlfriends. Of course, this happens all the time so that would be a lame excuse. He would cross that bridge when he came to it but for now it was time to go to dinner. As they passed through the revolving doors of the Stroganoff Steak House, Bill imagined every eye in the house was staring at the leopard woman and the old guy with her. It was a big place but designed in such a way to make every dining area unique with different styles of chairs and tables with an ambiance not unlike a private discreet place similar to the Francois Café in Delmarva. The aroma of steaks cooking was intoxicating to the senses and if romance was what you had in mind later, this was a great place to start. She ordered a bottle of Russian champagne and Bill understood how potent it could be as he remembered from his time with Svetlani at Chincoteague. Next was the cabbage stew and hot black bread followed by Chateaubriand steaks with a side order of beef stroganoff smothered in porto sauce. No Russian dinner is ever complete without dessert, and no dessert is more popular than the Napoleon pastry.

As they walked out those revolving doors he could feel the stares again, but it is not so unusual for Russian women to dress up in stylish dresses. Yet, her outfit would be considered over the top even in Russia, and Bill wondered if they would allow her to even enter the Hermitage

Theater which was their next destination. It didn't matter because when they arrived there, she walked in like she was Empress Elizabeth and who was going to challenge Peter the Great's daughter in this city that he founded? It was a delightful performance of Swan Lake and the supporting orchestra and when the performance concluded the cast received thundering applause and several standing ovations.

When they got back to the hotel after the fantastic performance, he had almost forgotten about all that had transpired earlier in the day regarding his interview with Ms. Brumel and the ride back to the hotel with her and Olga. Olga was tired and sleepy and as they took the elevator to the eighth floor, he was hoping she would invite him into her room because his desire for her was so overwhelming and all the other concerns even for his own safety no longer mattered.

She was so seductive and enticing his only thought was to assist in removing her mini-dress, blouse, panties and bra and then snuggle up to her until morning. His thoughts were quickly smothered when she told him a hug and kiss would have to do for now. Although it had been a hellishly long day, he was not ready to go to bed, needing a glass of Russian champagne to calm his nerves and help him relax. He had several of them at the Stroganoff Steakhouse earlier in the evening but that was over five hours ago so he took the elevator down to the lobby bar and ordered one and sat at a small table with two chairs.

Vera Petrova, Love of His Life

He spotted a "lady of the night" sitting next to two guys at the bar and she immediately looked his way. He was only there a few minutes when she came over and asked if he wanted some company and without really giving it much thought, he said it would be fine and offered to buy her a drink. She accepted and before long, they were engaged in conversation with mainly Bill answering questions about life in the USA.

After about 20 minutes, it became apparent that they liked each other. Up to now, she did not mention why she had been sitting at a bar at 1am with two guys so Bill decided to inquire why she left them and came over to his table.

"After about 10 minutes talking to them, I concluded that they were not the type of guys I want to be with for two hours or for that matter even 15 minutes." But Bill was a little puzzled since they were well dressed and appeared to be well groomed. "I didn't like their attitude or their offer wanting me to please both of them at the same time with certain types of sex acts that included hand cuffs, rope and chain. They turned me off completely since I believe only in conventional sex although I do oral but only with one man at a time."

At this point, Bill had to explain that he wasn't here to make any offer to go to bed with anyone since there was a lady in the room next to him who was his traveling companion and gave him strict orders on who not to associate with. "I know the type of woman you are talking about who thinks the world is her oyster and she is better than anyone else."

"And now is the time for me to ask you some questions? What is your name and how did you learn to speak such fluent English and tell me a little bit about your family."

"My name is Vera Petrova, I have a 17 year old son attending school in London, and two elderly and ailing parents who I love dearly and I am 38 years old. The reason I love my parents so much is because they sent me to language school when I was eight years old where I was in classes where only English was allowed to be spoken. I do this gig twice a month because I need the money but I choose my clients very carefully. I own my van and during the day I am a tour guide. Is there anything else you'd like to know?"

When Bill looked at the clock, it was almost 2am and he was totally exhausted when he felt her foot move up his inner leg. "Look Vera, you are a very attractive woman and I would love to share a bed with you but not this morning. Are you available for a tour of the city sometime after 12 noon tomorrow? I will pay you for an entire day but I need to sleep until at least 10am. I want to learn more about you and I insist on giving you some rubles for the time you spent with me."

At this time, tears were pouring from her eyes and she said she would love to be with him tomorrow and would be in the lobby at the time specified. They hugged as if they were already good friends and as he walked to the elevator, he was singing to himself because he felt he had really met someone very special. He and Olga had already decided to take the next day off to be independent of each other and catch up on their personal matters and just rest.

He had guessed right because it was 10:15am when he awoke and after taking his shower and getting a bite to eat, it was 11:45 and when he sat down to wait on Vera, he spotted her coming through the revolving door and she was indeed a woman who possessed all the physical assets and as she walked toward him, he opened his arms and they embraced. He was almost speechless when she took his hand and said, "Follow me." She led him to her van and asked where he wanted to start. She had a quiet confidence and charm that one might not notice at first but after just one hour with her last night, he understood that this lady was not only kind, responsible and sincere but someone you just wanted to be around. They decided that the Peter and Paul Cathedral and Fortress would be a good place to start the afternoon.

On the way there, Bill was anxious to hear more about her family, especially her 17 year old son. She explained that early on in his elementary school years, his teachers recognized that he was a talented and gifted young boy and recommended him to attend the schools that were set up by the government to provide the proper education for these future leaders in industry. Russia is rich in natural resources and hundreds of new energy companies were being formed, and the need for executive officers was acute.

The government paid for all his early education and training while in Russia but when he decided he wanted to attend a prestigious business school in London, the monthly stipend they provided was woefully inadequate so she had no choice but to do the twice a month gig that she certainly wasn't proud of but felt she had little choice. Her parents were living off a meager pension which she had to augment. Every morning before her tour, she would go by to check on them in their government subsidized apartment. As they pulled into the parking area, she rushed over to open the door for him, taking his hand as if she was proud to be with this old guy. With all her responsibilities it did not dampen her enthusiasm one iota. Her upbeat personality and confident demeanor gave him a sense of comfort he was badly in need of.

He had not seen Olga since he walked her to her door after their dinner and theater engagement the night before. She was probably using today to catch up on her rest but also to write a report for her agency, the RIS.

This was only conjecture on his part, but he could not erase from his mind Olga's involvement in all the strange things going on around him. But now he was with Vera and wanted to forget all this. As they walked toward the Cathedral holding hands, he was thinking he had found a real soul-mate. The Peter and Paul Fortress and Cathedral are on an island by the name of Zayachy close to the Neva River. The Fortress has quite a history of its own housing prisoners such as Alexander, the brother of Lenin and Peter the Great's own rebellious son, but it was the Cathedral Bill was interested in for today since their time on the island would be limited.

This is where all the Tsars are laid to rest (except Peter 2) and when you see the crypts of Peter the Great, Empress Elizabeth and Catherine the Great, your mind can't help but to wonder back to the early history of this great city and the contribution they all made in its formative decades. Inside the Cathedral, there is St. Catherine's Chapel and underneath its floor lies the remains of Tsar Nicholas 2, his family and servants. When Lenin and his comrade's took control of the country in 1917, they were sent into exile in the city of Yekaterinburg near the Ural Mountains. While living in a place called the Ipatiev House, the Bolsheviks sent their henchmen to slaughter them as they were herded into the basement where they were shot and stabbed with bayonets. They were buried in a shallow grave outside the city until 1998 when their remains were exhumed and brought here to be with all their relatives and predecessors.

When they ended the tour, Bill and Vera walked back to her van hand in hand and before she started her motor, she took his hand and placed it on her thigh. "Bill, I can't stand the thought that after today we may never have a chance to be together again." At this point, tears came into both of their eyes, embracing tightly for what seemed like an hour. He understood her concern and he had to find some more time to be with her, not only for this period of time but in the future.

Looking for a way to extend their day, she suggested they have dinner at The White Cat, Black Cat since it was near the Smolny Cathedral and would be an opportunity to see another important landmark in this city of splendor. As they approached the imposing blue and white structure, Vera said it was originally built to be the house of Peter the Great's daughter Elizabeth when she decided to become a nun after being passed over in the succession order. After her predecessor was deposed and she became Empress, it was mainly used to store her hundreds of gowns. It was said she never wore the same gown twice during her many years on the throne. While there, they got a bystander to take some pictures of them in various poses and there was little doubt they enjoyed being together.

As they walked into The White Cat, Black Cat, they were acting like two honeymooners. It was like they could not get enough of each other, and he decided that if she suggested extending the evening into his bedroom, he would enthusiastically accept but now it was time for dinner. It was a cozy place to eat and their dish of the day was roasted wild pheasant and potatoes in a cabbage broth served with a Russian favorite of homemade black bread right out of the oven. They both decided this was what they wanted and washed it all down with a carafe of house wine.

In a way, it reminded him of the roasted pork roast Olga's mother Marina prepared when they were in Kostroma. When they got into Vera's van for the trip back to the hotel, the hour was getting late. He placed his hand on her inner thigh as she had requested earlier. He understood well what a delightful lady Vera was, and he could not let her go without demonstrating in some meaningful way how very much she meant to him. There was little question that Vera was a very attractive woman but what impressed him most was her intellectual and spiritual being. Her overwhelming commitment to her son made certain he would have the tools required to succeed in the highly competitive business world. Also, she cared enough about her mum and dad to check on them every morning to be sure they took their medicine and got a nutritious breakfast.

Up to now, she did not talk about the father of her son or any of her pasts and he was not about to ask. So he decided to approach her with this question while still holding his hand on her inner thigh, "Would you ever consider marrying again?" Of course when he asked her the question he had to assume she'd been married previously and she answered in this way, "If I found that one in a million guy I would consider it and age would not be a factor. I would rather marry an older man and have a happy ten year marriage than marry a younger one who was always on the prowl."

With that, they pulled into the parking lot of the Azimut Hotel and he asked if she would consider coming into the hotel bar for a nightcap. "No Bill, but if we can take a bottle of champagne to your room, I will be more than happy to be with you." This time, he was more than happy to accept her offer, knowing they would have to pass Olga's room to get to his, but he was willing to accept the consequences.

When they got to his room, he immediately put the "Do not disturb" sign on the outer knob and the next move he would leave to Vera. She had brought her night bag from her van and asked him if she could take a shower and change into something more comfortable. "Of course, make yourself right at home" was his quick response and the anticipation of what was to follow was spine chilling and he couldn`t wait to see what she had in mind.

After about five minutes in the shower, she asked Bill to join her there. Since the shower heads were the hand held variety, she whispered to him in her teasing dialect, "I'll hold it for you and you can hold it for me." After hearing her invitation, it took him less time than it would take Bolt to run the 100 meters to join her. After seeing her in the nude, he wondered how any man could resist her advances if they were to have a preview.

She was more beautiful than he had imagined with rounded full breasts, a flat stomach and legs like Olga. And now her seductive smile gave him a rush of blood and it was easy for her to see that he was ready for any action she requested. He was as proud of it as he was when he was a 20 year old. She then handed him a bar of scented soap. "Soap me down good Bill, and I will do the same for you." Moving his hands over her soft body while she was doing the same for him felt so heavenly he didn't want to rush into any premature action. She seemed pleased to see that he had a full erection and after soaping it good, she ran a spray of warm water over it and then knelt down and gave the head a French kiss looking up to say, "I love you, Bill."

Wow!!! Those four words were music to his ears because he wanted to spend the remainder of his life with her. To find a woman who possessed all the qualities a man could possibly want or desire was even better than finding "a diamond in the rough."

She had said earlier she would consider marrying an older man but was the age gap between them too great? "Now Bill, let's dry each other off and I will pour you a glass of champagne after which we will get under the sheets and the fun will really begin. And don't worry if it gets a little soft, I will get it back up for you."

Her words alone were enough to bring a man to his knees and as they got into bed, he was almost in a state of frenzy. She removed the top sheet and invited him to use her body in any way he wished. He first used his tongue to lick her hardened nipples, and then caressed her vulva and inner thighs. She was what womanhood was all about and he began to wonder how he could ever live without her.

He turned her over and spent some precious moments on the back side of her thighs and cheeks. It was a titillating experience he would never forget and then he heard these words, "You have given me everything a woman dreams of when she is having a meaningful relationship and now it is my time to please you. Feel free to guide me and tell me what your desires are because when you love someone as I love you, bringing you happiness is what I am all about." The champagne was having its effect and now she asked him to moisten her vagina with his tongue and what happened after that is only a memory because he was now in some dreamland he had never visited before.

It was 7am when he awoke and they were in a full embrace. He remembered her telling him about his potency and a real gusher and then cleaning him up with a warm washcloth and towel. While lying there, he understood that in less than 48 hours, he and Olga would be boarding the Sapsan bullet train for the last leg of their journey and the thought of leaving St. Petersburg and never seeing Vera again was too sad to even contemplate. He had not seen Olga for over 36 hours and he had forgotten what they had on their schedule for today.

When Vera came out of her slumber she planted two well-placed kisses on his inner thighs and reminded him that she had to leave to look in on her mom and dad. Checking on them was her morning call to duty and that was just one more reason he thought so much of her. She insisted on doing another shower together before leaving and when she observed that she had excited him again, she laughed and before leaving she had given him his third full release in just seven hours and marveled that a man his age could have all that staying power. While Vera was getting dressed, he placed 30 thousand rubles near her night bag and when she saw it, she protested vociferously and refused to accept it. He explained to her in these words, "The money is not for the time you provided to me over the past 18 hours, but instead for the education you have given me about the importance of taking care of your loved ones no matter the sacrifice to yourself."

"I am not a wealthy man but I have ample funds and income to live out my life comfortably. I insist you tuck it away in your night bag or I will refuse to walk you to your van." With that, she kissed him on the lips and they held hands as they walked to the elevator and then to her van. "Bill, is there any way we can be together before you leave for Moscow Friday morning?" And without even thinking about what was on his schedule, he said, "Yes, can you meet me in the parking lot tomorrow evening at 7pm?" She didn't hesitate one minute in agreeing and they embraced one more time before she drove away.

The Neva River Cruise

It was now 9am on Wednesday and he remembered that he and Olga had signed up for a cruise on the Neva River for 5pm this evening. Although there was much going on in his personal life, it was an opportunity to see St. Petersburg from a different vantage point. There were still eight hours before their meeting and after spending the night with Vera, he just wanted to be alone for a while to organize his thoughts and enjoy the memories of the glorious time they had spent together.

As he walked from the parking lot to the lobby the desk clerk, whom he remembered as the young lady who kindly helped him find the newspaper article pertaining to Mikhail's accident, motioned for him to come over. She explained that a lady who identified herself as Irina Koslovovich who said she was the sister of Mikhail wanted to talk to him and she was sitting in the lobby. "She is the lady in the yellow dress with the blue-rimmed glasses reading the newspaper."

If she was really the sister of Mikhail, he would be more than glad to talk to her, but what if she was a "plant" sent there by the RIS? As he slowly walked over to introduce himself, he would have to be at the top of his game mentally. Vigilance and patience would be necessary if he were to avoid falling into a trap.

"Good morning Ms. Koslovovich. I have been informed that you would like to speak to me." With a smile on her face, she rose to her feet, "Oh yes, Mr. Bond, it is so nice to meet you, even though my brother only knew you a short while you must have made a great impression on him. He called me from the smoking car early that morning to tell me what time he would be at my apartment." At this time Bill needed to ask her two questions. "Did he call about 6am and was his breathing strained?" She responded, "Yes to both and I asked him if he was feeling okay and said he thought he had come in contact with the flu virus."

Bill was gaining confidence that she was indeed Mikhail's sister and he was becoming intensely interested in everything she had to say. Bill explained that the night before Mikhail was very lucid and upbeat and was looking forward to visiting her but by morning, he seemed pale and his breathing was heavy.

They reinforced their belief that he did not jump on to the tracks and take his own life. Bill was more puzzled than ever and asked if Mikhail was a smoker. "No, two things our parents made us understand early were to stay away from tobacco and alcohol and learn the English language. He told me he came to the outside platform to get some fresh air and was going to remain there until he got to St. Petersburg."

Bill did not mention the note Mikhail had given to him before leaving the cabin just in case he was wrong about Ms. Koslovovich although he was 99% sure she was not an RIS informant. At 60 years old Mikhail seemed to be in good health and Bill was becoming more convinced he was the victim of foul play. Bill could not erase from his mind that Olga had something to do with this. They exchanged e-mail addresses and would keep in touch if either learned anything new regarding the now deceased Mikhail. After spending the night with Vera and meeting Ms. Koslovovich, Bill was dead tired and decided to go to his room and try to take a nap before his 5pm appointment with Olga.

Lying there, he could hardly believe the chain of events that had taken place in his life since he met Olga at a restaurant in Delmarva, USA. It all started before when he read an article that advised retired older guys not to be afraid to flirt with the ladies if they want to have a more interesting and happier retirement. And now he was in a room in St. Petersburg, Russia wondering if it was all worth it and it certainly was since he had met Vera here. Also, all the other wonderful people he had met in Kostroma like Marina, Andrey, Kira and Luba and of course Anthony. Yes, when he first heard that there was an Anthony, he was envious and jealous but now things had taken a dramatic change.

He had set the alarm for 4:30pm and he must have dozed off because when it rang, he couldn't remember why he had set it.

As he sat up on the side of his bed, he finally cleared his mind and remembered he was to meet Olga in the lobby at 5pm for their Neva River cruise. When they did the early planning of their itinerary, it was something he was looking forward to and despite his mind thinking of hardly anything else but Vera Petrova he was anxious to go. When he got to the lobby, Olga was waiting, dressed in dark slacks and red sweater, she was as beautiful as ever except her face looked strained.

It had been many hours since he had last seen her and the ride to the port was one of quiet reflection for both as they hardly spoke. It was obvious that something was bothering her. They had designated this day to be independent of the other until 5pm and he imagined she was taking care of some RIS business.

But now they were boarding the Gondola that would take them up the Neva River and into the many canals to view the architectural wonders of this city of endless splendor. You wish you could get into one of those fabled time machines and be with those artisans who were planning and laying out this treasured piece of real estate in the early 18ᵗʰ century. They sometimes compare it to Venice but having been there, St. Petersburg was his pick of the two.

He had noticed on one of the structures the year 1732 engraved in its marble and being well versed in American history, it was the year of George Washington's birth, our first President. He was credited with laying out the capital of the USA, Washington, D.C. And Bill could not help but wonder if George had gotten some of his ideas from this historic venue. Bill's mind was so filled with these thoughts of the past he had almost forgotten that Olga was sitting across from him. She seemed to sense that he was in full appreciation of what he was taking in and didn't want to interrupt.

Of course he would have given "a penny for her thoughts" because it was obvious that she was in a deep state of reflection. He would have to wait to break the ice and begin some kind of dialog. After all, this was her country, and he was her guest.

Their two-hour cruise was ending, and as they de-boarded they decided to go into the nearby pastry shop for a mug of hot chocolate and donut while waiting for their taxi.

She broke her silence by telling Bill that a Swedish ship would be coming into port in the morning, and one of her "pasts" was onboard, and that he had called to ask if they could spend the day together.

"Bill, I am asking for your understanding because I realize that tomorrow is our last day in St. Petersburg, and we had a busy day planned, but I had little choice but to say yes to his request. You see, some years ago I was in serious financial distress and he helped me with a loan which I agreed to pay back in both money and time. I haven't completely paid back the loan by his calculations, and he promised me that after tomorrow the debt would be settled."

Bill was stunned beyond words, and when he finally absorbed the meaning of her admission he responded. "Now Olga, you know this is not a matter of asking for my understanding, because you know it isn't about us anymore, but your relationship with Anthony. Did you inform him of your intentions?" She seemed indignant that he would ask her, and she responded. "Anthony and I have a very mature relationship, and whether I choose to inform him or not is strictly my business."

He was completely surprised with her answer and all he could say was "In that case I think you should go with your past lover." There was a look of anger on her face, and no doubt she didn't like the term "past lover."

"You are trying to portray me as some cheap whore and frankly, I resent it." With that, the taxi outside was blowing his horn and on the ride back to the hotel, a cold chill had developed between them and as they walked into the lobby, she realized that Bill had been deeply affected and knowing the Moscow end of their journey was still ahead, she asked if he would like to come to her room for a couple of hands of blackjack. He was also sorry he had used the term "past lover" so he accepted her invitation knowing there was little chance of any sexual activity between them anymore.

More Time with Vera

With that, they took the elevator to the 8th floor and he told her he would need to go to his room for about 20 minutes before joining her. When he closed the door to his room, he immediately called Vera and asked if there was any chance they could spend the entire day together tomorrow instead of just the 7pm meeting they had already arranged. She couldn't have been happier and said she would look after her parents in the morning, and they agreed that 10am would be good for both of them.

After their conversation, he went over to Olga's room and knocked on the door. She had taken off her dark slacks and red sweater and was now wearing a revealing negligee, "I hope you don't mind me slipping into my nighties to be more comfortable." He didn't want to spoil this period of "forgive and forget" and told her he didn't mind at all, having confidence now he could turn back any offer to go to bed if that was her intent. They sat down on the edge of her bed as she began to shuffle the blackjack cards. He had developed a hard on and wasn't sure whether it was from looking at her breasts or thinking about his meeting with Vera tomorrow.

After about 35 minutes with her winning a few rubles, Bill stood up, kissed her on the forehead and said he would meet her on Friday morning in the lobby at 7am. She seemed a little disappointed that Bill ended the blackjack session a bit early and he was sure she expected him to make an overture to spend at least some part of the night under the sheet as they had done at Chincoteague.

Whether she would have agreed to his overture is pure conjecture because she always found a reason why it was not the right time to repeat their experience at Chincoteague. It was probably a blow to her self-confidence when he decided not to make a move, but maybe she needed a lesson in humility although there was little doubt about her sexual attractiveness.

When he removed his clothes to go to bed, he still had a hard on and was in need of some relief so he laid down thinking only of Vera and was able to obtain a full release. When he awoke the next morning, he could think only of Vera and their 10am meeting. After his shower and breakfast, he went outside where the air was cool and invigorating, and decided to take a walk in the small park next to the parking lot where he knew Vera would be arriving in her van shortly.

It was funny because there was a pretty lady walking in front of him throwing left jabs and right crosses as if she were training for some future boxing match. He understood that this was a form of "power walking" and he had heard it was much better than actual running for burning calories and keeping in shape. And maybe those punches were meant to vent her anger at some person maybe she didn't like… perhaps her boss. Soon, Bill got into the spirit of the moment throwing some pretty mean punches of his own and when she looked back, she realized he was emulating her, giving him a smile as if to say, "I am glad I am having a positive influence on you."

When they rounded the horseshoe bend on the walking track, Bill spotted Vera's van pulling into the adjacent parking lot and wanting to get there before she could walk to the lobby, he quickened his pace from a power walk to a sprint, passing the nice lady in front of him, smiling back at her as she had done earlier to him.

His timing was perfect because when he got to her van, she had just gotten out and seeing him they embraced like teenage sweethearts. It was at that time his walking mate came by and muttered something in Russian he could not understand and he asked Vera to interpret it for him and she laughed saying, "No wonder you were so giddy and silly, obviously being reunited with your long lost granddaughter." They both laughed and Bill didn't feel too bad because although she was 38, she could easily pass for 25.

It would be just 24 hours before leaving for Moscow but today it would be just the two of them and he wanted it to be a special day for Vera. "Well, Bill, where would you like to start?" It could be a hundred places to start in this city of many choices but being fascinated with Lenin, he wanted to go to the Finland Rail Station. It was here that Lenin returned from exile from Germany on April 3, 1917 and gave a rousing speech to the masses imploring them to rise up against their masters and landowners and seize their properties.

It was the beginning of what was to be known as the October Revolution and although there was infighting among the various factions the Bolsheviks emerged as the victors and they deposed Nicholas 2, and sent him and his family into exile to Yekaterinburg where they were eventually slaughtered like cattle in the basement of their quarters.

The locomotive that brought Lenin to the station still stands on a piece of track with the number 293 emblazoned on the front. An imposing statue of Lenin is standing at the entrance to the station and, interestingly, a few people had planted explosives at its base in 2009, but all they accomplished was to leave a huge hole in the ground. And when Vera remarked it was a stupid thing to do because whether you despised him or loved him, he was part of Russian history and trying to pretend the 1918 revolution didn't happen or Lenin's role in it was to ignore reality.

She had an excellent grasp of Russian history, but being in the trade that caters to tourists from all countries she was careful to keep her inner thoughts and beliefs to herself. Their next stop would be the Summer Garden and as they walked its tree lined walks and paths hand in hand, it was the perfect place to relax and forget your troubles. Now and then they would stop and rest on one of the benches provided, with Vera insisting on a hug and kiss each time.

Of course Bill was more than happy to be the recipient of all this attention. They were now in close proximity to the spot where it was said Peter the Great sketched out on a piece of parchment a drawing of what he wanted the park and Summer Palace to look like. They walked a little farther to an area where a musical fountain was surrounded by statues and busts of notables of the past and you got a feeling that they were alive and you are a part of history.

They made brief stops at St. Michaels Cathedral, The Alexander Garden and The Admirality and Hermitage each time Vera giving Bill a fascinating story about an interesting part of the history of each place. They had started the day at 10am and it was now 6pm and they were both in need of a good meal. And Vera knew just where to go and she chose a place called the Restoran. She explained it was an all you can eat feast of small sample dishes of food and morsels of all kind which is called The Zakuski or Russian Table. It is truly an experience that all visitors to St. Petersburg should not miss. It is a smorgasbord of delectable fish, meat, vegetables, breads, pastries and desserts that would satisfy even the most discriminating appetite. Bill could not get over how lucky he was to have met Vera.

It was now 7:15pm and even though he had to get up early the next morning to meet Olga and take a taxi to the train depot he wanted to extend the day with Vera as long as possible. He wondered if Olga had a long day with her "past" but he probably would not see her until it was time for them to meet in the lobby at 8am Friday morning. Vera said she would stay with him in his room until midnight although she was booked in the morning to take an elderly couple from Israel on a tour to Peterhof.

After their feast, they drove back to the hotel and as they entered the lobby hand in hand, there sat Olga in a chair with her eyes fixated on both of them. At this time, she was the last person he wanted to see, not only because he hoped to keep his relationship with Vera private but because she would probably want to have a little discussion about their upcoming trip to Moscow. In fact, he was sure that is why she was perched in her chair waiting for his return. It was an awkward situation but his job now was to introduce them.

"Vera, I want you to meet my good friend Olga, who extended an invitation to me to visit Russia and without her encouragement, I probably would not be here. Olga, this is my special friend Vera." With that, Vera, being a very unpretentious and sincere woman, did not understand the full implications of her actions when she leaned over to hug Olga.

"Oh it is so nice to meet you and I can't thank you enough because Bill is a very special man and I can't adequately express the amount of joy he has given me over the short few days and nights I have known him." Knowing how Olga reacted to Dasha Brumel's flirtatious ways, he tried to change the subject. "And Olga, how did your day go with your friend from the Swedish ship?"

"We had a great time and as a matter of fact, I will be going to dinner with him shortly so I am so sorry I will have to leave now," shaking the hand of Vera as she walked briskly out the revolving doors presumably to meet this guy or just take a walk to kill some time.

Knowing Olga well, he could tell from her quick exit and the change in her facial color that the trip to Moscow tomorrow would not be a pleasant one. But Vera didn't seem to notice anything unusual about her quick exit by commenting how beautiful she was and wishing she had met her earlier. But that was typical for Vera, because she had the kind of disposition where she had very little time for jealousy and mistrust.

But she was a very curious person and almost innocently asked him how he had met Olga and whether any romance had taken place during their friendship.

"No, there was an understanding from the start that she had finally met the man of her dreams and after many earlier disappointments he was the only guy she had any interest in from a physical point of view. I met him in Kostroma and he is a real gentleman and his name is Anthony."

Of course this was not an honest statement and Bill was already feeling guilty, but sometimes at the spur of the moment, it is not the time to be candid as long as you set the record straight later when there is more time to explain the kinds of things that happened at Chincoteague the day of the big storm. He did explain that they had met at a restaurant in the USA in the summer of last year while she was waiting tables there. It was now time to go to his room where just the two of them could be together for the next few hours.

As they passed Olga's room, he now knew that she would be aware that Vera would be keeping him busy for some time this evening, so he could only guess what kind of lecture he would be getting in the morning if she discovered that Vera was a prostitute.

In Bill's mind, Vera was a wonderful woman and he did not think of her that way because he knew she was a kind, considerate and responsible mother and daughter and a woman he would marry in a minute if she would have him. He still had the champagne and glasses in his small room refrigerator from the last time Vera visited him and after having a glass they repeated all the touching, caressing and lovemaking that had taken place a few nights earlier.

Since she would be leaving at midnight he mainly wanted to talk about their possible future together. He could not bear the thought that when he left tomorrow, she would be making love with someone else later in the month when her funds were low. He knew this was the only woman he could be happy with and asked her to hold off on any future engagements until he got back to the USA. "I love you and I will send you a monthly stipend to cover not only your loss from your two engagements but an extra 3000 rubles to buy something for you."

"You have given so much to others and it is about time to give to yourself." With that, she put her arms around him, "Bill, I love you more than you will ever know and I have no desire to make love to anyone but you. You are a very generous man and I will wait for whatever time you need to get your personal life in order. I will marry you tomorrow if you ask me. I know that is not possible because of your schedule."

"Tell Olga I said goodbye and hope we can spend some time together in the future." It was now time for them to put their clothes back on and walk to Vera's van and when they got there they embraced and neither wanted to let go because the future was so uncertain. She was Russian and he was an American, she was young and he was old but yet there was a common thread that brought them together. He met her by chance on the evening he and Olga had just returned from dinner and the theater. As she drove away, the tears were streaming from his eyes because when you meet someone like her, you should never have to part.

As he walked back into the hotel and to his room, he wondered if Olga had returned from her dinner engagement with her ex-past. If what she told him was true, she would no longer be indebted to him or had she made it all up. He wished he could spend the rest of his time in Russia with Vera right here in St. Petersburg. When he went to bed, he could only think of Vera but he knew when he awoke in the morning, he and Olga would be checking out. And morning came very quickly.

Back to Moscow on Sapsan

When he went to breakfast, Olga was already there having her usual cup of tea and pastry, reading the newspaper. Trying to initiate a conversation, he asked if that was all she was going to eat since it would be a long time before they arrived at the Katerina Park Hotel in Moscow where they had made reservations while spending the night there when he arrived in Moscow two weeks earlier.

"They will be serving a nice lunch on Sapsan and for the price they charge for a ticket, they could afford to provide a gourmet meal. I am sure that woman Vera gave you a good workout last night so you will need a hearty breakfast." She then excused herself saying she had to attend to some last minute items and would meet him outside near the taxi stand in 45 minutes.

On the taxi ride over to the depot, Olga engaged in conversation with the driver in Russian while Bill enjoyed getting his last good look at a city he had learned to love in the short time he had been here. Yes there were many disappointments regarding Mikhail but when Vera entered his life, everything changed for him. Now, they were boarding the Sapsan bullet train and in three hours, they would be in Moscow. The attendant checking passports welcomed Bill to her country and wished him a happy and comfortable journey to Moscow. Russian women have an unmistakable face profile and she was a knockout.

Soon he and Olga would be sitting in a four seat compartment facing each other and before they could speak a word, almost unbelievably, Parker Standish arrived and claimed one of the remaining two seats. Although she was very opinionated, they gave her a friendly reception and both expressed their sincere welcome. After all, they had spent 17 hours with her on the train ride from Kostroma to St. Petersburg and even though she exhibited some English stuffiness, she was really a nice woman.

Almost immediately, she began to talk about Mikhail's "unpleasant departure" as she worded it and the bad treatment she received from the Russian interrogator. She described him as an old communist leftover from the Stalinist era and it was obvious he didn't care for her and she damn sure didn't show any respect for him. "I didn't give them any information other than to tell them Mikhail was a real gentleman and Russia needed more men like him and less like the ones I've met recently." She quipped that probably in the old days they would have taken her passport and sent her to Siberia. Even Olga got a laugh from that remark. Soon the last person came to take the remaining seat in their four seat compartment. It was apparent he was not going to be the outgoing type, immediately opening his laptop, without even a gesture to the other three that they were even present. Parker seemed to understand that her usual banter was not going to go over well with him. He was all business and had no interest in engaging in conversation of any kind. In a way, it was much appreciated by Olga who was still trying to absorb all that had taken place in St. Petersburg.

To take some of the pressure off her, Bill thought about offering to relieve her of the burden of the commitments they had made for the Moscow leg of the trip. Although Anthony was the main guy in her life, she seemed to be jealous that other attractive ladies enjoyed, his company and he was paying less attention to her. On the night they played blackjack in her room when she dressed in her sexy nighties and he pretended not to notice had to be a real downer for a woman who was the very epitome of womanhood.

Riding on Sapsan was a stimulating experience because you got the sensation you were traveling at a high rate of speed but yet it was almost like you were floating on air. And the good food and excellent service made it all worthwhile even though you were paying a hefty premium for the ticket. When they arrived in Moscow, they got a taxi to take them to the same hotel where they had spent one night a fortnight ago when he arrived here, the Katerina Park Hotel. They agreed to go to their separate rooms for a few hours to take care of their personal stuff but would meet at 8pm for drinks and dinner at the hotel restaurant. He remembered the meal they enjoyed two weeks earlier and was looking forward to the dinner hour, but his first priority was to send an e-mail to Vera. So he sat down and penned this letter…

"My Dear Vera, It was a very pleasant trip on the Sapsan bullet train and I am looking forward to my time in Moscow because of its history as a very important and prestigious world capital. I considered myself a very lucky man to have met you, and the time we spent together these past several days will always be a precious and unforgettable memory for me. I know our age difference has to be an important consideration for you and I will respect any decision you make regarding the future. When I get back to the USA next week, I will send you the funds I promised and formalize a proposal that I made to you verbally. I love you and miss you already. Bill"

She must have been expecting his letter because almost immediately, she wrote back. "I know our time together was short but I was able to recognize that you are a very responsible and caring guy. I will be most happy to wait for you and I will gladly accept all the terms of your proposal. You are young of heart and that is all that matters to me. I love you very, very much. Vera"

Bill was so delighted to hear from Vera that he began to hum one of his favorite oldies… "Ain't no mountain high enough, ain't no valley low enough to keep me from getting to you baby… to keep me from getting to you." He took the elevator to the dining room and Olga was already sitting at a table in the back corner. This would be the first time they could have a conversation without someone else being present and it didn't take her long to get things "off her chest" so to speak.

She first apologized for canceling their day in St. Petersburg to be with her "past" but under the circumstance she had no choice. Without really thinking, he told her it turned out great for him because it gave him some extra time to be with Vera. This really infuriated Olga and without hesitation she asked, "Did you know her before we arrived in St. Petersburg and did you have sex with her?"

He was surprised by her sudden intrusion into his privacy but he responded, "I just met her this past week and yes, we shared the same bed together for two nights." This made her even angrier and now her Russian temper was gaining steam. "Do you remember when we first arrived in St. Petersburg and we were having a glass of wine in the lobby when you expressed the wish to kiss and caress me from head to toe as we had done at Chincoteague and yet when I invited you to my room to play blackjack, you showed no interest in pursuing your desire?" At this time the server appeared at their table and he was spared from answering a very delicate question at least for the moment.

They both decided to have the special of the evening which was their steak and salmon combination in a savory sauce containing ten herbs and spices as only Russian chefs are capable of preparing. After the server had taken their order, she was still relentless to get an answer from him regarding his failure to respond to her previous question. "I was totally exhausted that night and didn't want to take the chance of a poor performance because of lack of energy" was the only answer he could think of.

She looked at him sheepishly as if to say you had your opportunity and I am damn sure not going to give you another chance to humiliate me. With that, they finished their glass of wine and retired for the evening in their separate rooms. They had a big day planned for tomorrow and in the morning they would take the metro from station "Pragskaya" only a five minute walk from the hotel.

The next morning, they had a most delightful buffet breakfast sharing the dining room with a very diverse group and the selections would satisfy just about every palate. When they got on the metro, Bill was fascinated with the various expressions on the faces of the passengers, some reading newspapers, some looking at their gadgets and others in deep thought and as he began to wonder about their personal lives, his eyes became fixated on a woman about 35 years of age whose face resembled his mother's when he was a boy of about 10.

He wondered if she too was on her way to some low paying domestic job just to earn a few rubles to put some food on the table for her children. The lines on her face and forehead made her appear to be much older than her actual biological age but this was typical for those whose lives were hardened by hard work and worry. When she got up at the next station to depart the train, Bill handed her a five thousand ruble note hoping it would make at least this week a little easier for her.

Olga had informed him that there would be seven stops before they would get to "Ohotny Ryad" which was their destination. When they arrived and stepped onto the platform, he was astounded by the opulent splendor of the place. Its marble walls and stairs, the bronze statues, the high ceiling with grandiose chandeliers left Bill in a state of wonderment. It was an achievement beyond imagination and one could spend a full day at this one stop without ever getting bored.

He noticed that some of the people passing through would rub a certain part of one of the bronze statues for good luck. One of his favorites was to see the guys rub the breasts of a beautiful woman of bronze, making her nipples stand out compared to the darker image of its entirety.

One could only imagine the enormous effort to construct the maze of tunnels and the 182 metro stations that made up the Moscow Metro System. And now it was time to take the escalators and steps to street level where they would spend some time exploring the grounds and structures in close proximity to Red Square. And once inside the square, the politburo would come to wave at the cheering crowds as the tanks and anti-aircraft guns passed underneath it was a surreal feeling. He remembered Stalin, Beria, Malenkov, in the old days of the 40's on up to Gorbachev, Yeltsin, Putin and Medvedev and all the others in between.

We were allies in the early years but in the 50's and 60's of the 20th century, things turned cold and the construction of the Berlin Wall only made relations between the two super powers worsen until Mikhail Gorbachev ordered its destruction in the mid 1980's and a new period of enlightenment followed which made it possible for Bill to be here today. Red Square is surrounded by structures like the huge department store

GUM (pronounced goom as in doom) and St. Basil's Cathedral and of course the Kremlin itself. GUM looks like a converted railroad station with its high ceiling and skylights and although today it is a shopping mecca of high prices for tourists, its history is fascinating.

At the turn of the century, it was a huge outdoor shopping area where 2500 stores and pavilions were located. In 1928, Stalin converted the building into an office complex to house his hundreds of planners, architects, and bureaucrats to implement his five year plan and the Metro System that Bill had just visited a few hours before was one of its great achievements in that period of their history. This was a day for just getting a look at some of the interesting places in the main part of Moscow and as the week progressed they would target specific places of interest to spend more time.

The Unforgettable Sergei

To save time, they decided to take a taxi back to the hotel instead of the metro. And this is when they discovered Sergei, their taxi driver who was truly a unique individual whose music defined the manner in which he would drive… sometimes fast and reckless and other times slow and serene. On this particular day, he preferred the more lively selections and as he zig-zagged through the heavy Moscow traffic at a high rate of speed.

Bill was already hoping they had chosen to take the Metro back instead. For most of the time, he kept his eyes closed and fingers crossed all the while listening to Sergei and Olga talking in Russian and he wondered if this was normal for Moscow. Olga always seemed to be flirting with dangerous situations and that is probably why she chose to be a spy. Maybe after Bill spurning her the night of blackjack she wanted to get even by scaring the hell out of the American sitting in the back seat. She chose to sit up front with Sergei perhaps to show him it was going to be a while before she would forgive him for that night and maybe his time with Vera was also on her mind. When the big sign on top of the roof was in sight, Katerina Park Hotel, he was greatly relieved. When Sergei went on his way, Bill asked her what in the world they found to talk about during such a stressful ride. "He proposed to take us on a night tour of Moscow this evening at a reduced rate." After escaping with their lives, there was no way he was ever going to get back in a taxi with that crazy guy.

But when Olga intimated that his age was making him a little timid and overly cautious, he knew it was her way of challenging his very manhood. So he decided to "throw caution to the wind" and instructed her to call Sergei and accept his offer but not at the reduced rate. The full rate is what they would pay. Sergei would be back to get them at 9:30pm.

It would provide enough time to take a shower and get a bite to eat and they decided to walk up to the shopping mall about ten minutes away where each ordered a grilled chicken sandwich and a bottle of Nestea. Bill found out quickly that the Nestea in Russia had a superior taste to what he was used to drinking in the USA. It had to be the superior waters from their deep springs. While there, they also stopped to get a few items at the stores in the mall. But now, it was getting close to the time when Sergei would return for their night tour of Russia, which both looked forward to.

It wasn't long into their trip when Bill realized that Sergei was someone he really liked a lot. The places they visited were too numerous to mention but The Great Church of Jesus Christ was perhaps the most beautiful and most interesting. It was fascinating because Lenin wanted to wipe out all the vestiges of religion in Russian culture. At least that is what we were taught in our schools in the USA. There was also a bridge on the property that led over the Moscow River and the view at night was absolutely stunning.

They travelled through the "tunnel of death" so named because to build it they had to tunnel under a cemetery and as they entered, Olga would say, "bye, bye it was nice to meet you" as if it were the tunnel of their death. The ride back to the hotel was fun and enjoyable and Bill would sing along in Russian with Sergei from the music he had chosen from his collection of CD's. Olga, whose educational background and social standing eclipsed both of them seemed to get a kick out of this old guy from the USA and this 35 year old Russian taxi driver having so much fun together.

By this time Bill was no longer fearful of Sergei's reckless driving because he understood he was a very skillful navigator and if he were in the United States, he could easily find a sponsor for the NASCAR circuit. Although it was very late when they returned to their hotel, Olga had mellowed considerably since getting back from St. Petersburg and they agreed to have a drink together before retiring to talk about their good time with Sergei. She had learned a lot about Sergei from their brief conversations during the night excursion. Having a troubled childhood, he resorted to petty theft at first, which proliferated into stealing cars. On his second jail term, he was befriended by one of the custodians who recognized that he was a good candidate for rehabilitation if he was given a decent opportunity. So, the custodian and his wife who was employed at the Russian consulate offered to give Sergei one of their used cars when he was released in a few months. They even suggested he might want to consider converting it into a taxi and they would help him secure his business license.

They let him know that if he chose to do this they were putting their reputations on the line. That was 18 years ago and Sergei not only took their advice, but also married a beautiful lady named Elena and they had two teenage children who were excelling in school. The custodian who put his trust in Sergei passed away one year ago and he told Olga that Bill reminded him of his friend and mentor. Bill, being a softie for this kind of thing found it difficult to keep the tears away. There was little doubt that a strong bond had developed between them.

It was now almost 1am when they decided to wrap things up for the evening and under different circumstances, this would have been an excellent opportunity to spend some quality time together either in her bed or his but after all that had transpired, it was no longer a viable choice.

Poison in Mikhail's Tissue

When Bill got to his room, he checked his e-mails and was shocked when he read this letter from Irina Koslovovich, the sister of Mikhail Popovich. "Dear Mr. Bond, I hope all is going well with you and I had promised if I heard any news regarding my brother, I would get in touch with you. Several days ago the authorities released Mikhail's body to our family. He had always told his children he wanted to be buried near our mom and dad at the family burial site outside St. Petersburg. But prior to the burial we decided to contact a good friend from Finland who happens to be a coroner to do an autopsy. He told us he detected lethal amounts of ciyanara in his tissue. He explained this deadly poison was developed by Soviet chemists in the 1940's on orders from Lavrent Beria. We have not yet made a decision on what to do regarding this painful revelation. Irina Koslovovich."

WOW!!! The implications of her letter not only affected their decision as a family but now being this close to Olga he began to wonder if he might be her next victim. Luckily the next day was to be a day of leisure because they decided to do another night tour with Sergei and wanted the day to rest. He could sleep in the next day but now he decided to go to various search engines across the world to learn as much as he could about ciyanara.

After about an hour with no luck he came across a search engine in Great Britain by the name of "diddle" run by operatives in the old Soviet system. Bill entered the word "ciyanara" on their site and got plenty of information. Joseph Stalin gave Lavrent Beria the task of developing a poison in the laboratories at Chelyabinsk which just happened to be where the Soviets were developing their germ warfare and nuclear research programs.

Many of their top scientists and chemists were located there. The chemists at Chelyabinsk were given the task of developing a poison that had the following characteristics... it must be deadly... it must be odorless... it must be soluble in any liquid... it must be a time release poison. Stalin and Beria were both from the province of Georgia and they wanted a way to deal with their foes without the messiness of the rope and bullet.

In other words, invite them to dinner, give them a pat on the back for doing a good job and then slip them a dose of ciyanara in their glass of vodka. It took about 14 months to develop the poison and was tested in the gulags on those who were given death sentences for crimes against the state. It was a powdery mixture kept in stainless steel vials with a screw off top in doses of 200mg. One dose was enough to kill a 250 lb. man within 12 hours and a 160 lb. man within 10 hours. The time release properties were timed to first attack the respiratory system and within eight to ten hours the intended victim would feel the need to get some fresh air. About 30 minutes later the nervous system would be affected and the victim would lose his equilibrium and his speech would be slurred and in the final stages it would enter the blood stream where certain death would occur within minutes.

It was now about 3am and Bill went into the bathroom to drench his face and eyes in cold water. He was now sure that Olga had delivered the tea that contained the poison around 10pm on the 17 hour train ride from Kostroma to St. Petersburg. Mikhail was breathing heavy when he left their cabin about 6am. He remembered they all were kidding Mikhail about getting the special cup with the nude lady imprinted on the outside.

Of course, that would be Olga's way of identifying the cup to be sure the poison was delivered to the intended victim. The time line fit perfectly but whether he fell or was pushed by one of Olga's comrades may never be known. The sixty four thousand dollar question is, why did he drink the tea? When he gave Bill the note, it proved he didn't trust Olga. But since he was sure she didn't recognize him, there was no reason to suspect she would do anything to upset Bill or Parker Standish. If that was his thinking it was a fatal mistake.

Earlier, when they stopped in the small town to buy some cookies, they all had tea while waiting for the rail workers to add some extra cars so why not have a bit before retiring for the evening. Some of these questions may never be answered but one thing Bill knew for sure he had to be alert and vigilant. He was feeling lonely when he sat down to send an e-mail to Vera Petrova. She would not get it for a couple hours since it was now just 4am. "My Dear Vera… It is 4 in the morning and I am here in my room at the Katerina Park Hotel in Moscow feeling very lonely. Last night we did a tour of Moscow which was most interesting but when I arrived back at my room, I received an e-mail which was quite disturbing. At this time, I can't divulge to you who sent it except to say I am becoming increasingly more suspicious of my traveling companion Olga who you met in the lobby of the Azimut. I am sending you a money order later today to cover your lost income for a year. When I get back to the USA, I will explain everything in detail. Love you very much, Bill."

When he awoke the next day it was noon and he was so happy that this was to be a day of leisure. It was too late for the breakfast buffet so he went up to the shopping mall to get a sandwich but before doing so, he checked his e-mails.

There was a letter from Vera, "My Dearest Bill, I am very upset at what you wrote to me. Why are you suspicious of Olga? During the few minutes when I met her she seemed very nice but maybe a little jealous. I need to know a little more about your situation because I am concerned and worried. I will be very busy today since I have two tours booked. You are so kind to send me a money order. When it arrives, I will deposit it in the bank for safekeeping. Please be careful and I will wait anxiously to hear from you. You are my one and only love, Vera."

As he walked toward the mall alone it was a strange feeling not having Olga in these situations. His Russian was limited and sometimes it was difficult to convey what he wanted. But by pointing to the picture of the item he was able to make the attendant understand he wanted a grilled cheese and salami sandwich.

After lunch, he walked over to the park and enjoyed a tennis match taking place between two very competitive men who appeared to be in their 40's. It was the one thing he noticed while in Russia when they designed neighborhoods they allowed ample space for a park like the one he was in now. After watching the match, he took a long walk all the while thinking on what his next move should be. He wanted to take the second night tour this evening with Sergei but he began to think of calling British Airways to arrange an early flight out of Moscow because now his safety was in question.

Tomorrow they were scheduled to go back to Red Square to visit places like St. Basel's Cathedral, the Armory, the Lenin Mausoleum and other places of interest they didn't have time for a few days ago. He decided to go back to his room and think things out and take a nap until Sergei arrived at 9:30pm. But going to sleep was very difficult with a hundred thoughts swirling in his mind. He wondered where Olga had spent the day and what she might be up to. He could not get her off his mind, thinking back to the time she appeared at their table at Hannah's and their near death experience at Chincoteague and their night at the Quality Inn where he touched and caressed every part of her body with his hand, lips and tongue. And then their dinner the last night in Delmarva and the ice cream place where they shared a banana split with one spoon. Her invitation to him to visit Russia with a veiled promise that they would share a bed and then when he arrived seeing her at the airport where she almost took his breath away because she was so beautiful standing there with outstretched arms to welcome him.

All those wonderful memories and now lying here on his bed he had reason to fear her. Maybe Shakespeare should have put it this way, "For love is blind and men fail to understand the evil trap she has set for him" He was now falling asleep so he set his alarm for 8:30pm, giving him an hour before Sergei's arrival.

Jealousy Rears its Head

When he awoke, he was glad because his dreams were not good ones. It was now time to take the elevator to the lobby for the night tour and when he arrived, she was standing there looking just as spectacular and sexy as he could ever remember. She embraced him and then spoke.

"Good evening Bill, I hope you enjoyed your day of leisure. I was in and out of the hotel all day and never saw you. I even knocked at your door a few times but got no response. By chance, did you take the Sapsan bullet train to St. Petersburg to see that Vera woman?"

He was surprised with her question because he actually considered doing that but when Vera wrote to him that she had two booked tours, it was not a viable option. But he decided to throw in a little levity.

"Yes that is exactly what I did and of all things, I was able to secure the room you had there, room 836." Bill continued with his tease, "The bed you had was comfortable but a little small but was perfect for our purposes and the two hours we spent there was like heaven on earth."

It was meant to be funny but when he saw the expression on her face, there was little doubt that she believed every word of it. It was a very possible thing to do, take the 7am Sapsan up, be at the hotel in St. Petersburg by noon, be with Vera for a few hours and take the 4pm Sapsan back to Moscow and still have time for a little rest prior to the 9:30pm appointment with Sergei.

Now her anger and jealousy were very evident, "I am very disappointed that you would do something like this considering our tour tonight with Sergei and our early departure in the morning for our trip to Red Square. I would think that you would want to be fully rested but it is obvious all you can think about are breasts and pussy."

This was getting to be fun and he decided to keep the conversation going, "Vera is a very special woman and I love and respect her very much and the trip was well worth the time and money."

By this time her Russian temper was running hot, "Oh bullshit Bill, just because she was willing to give you a fuck and blow job you are now ready to marry her. Whores like her are a dime a dozen in Russia and I am surprised you would lower yourself to her level. For Christ sake Bill, you have known her for about a week and for all you know, she might be a member of the Russian mafia."

This really hurt Bill and he felt it necessary to come to Vera's defense, explaining of all the sacrifices she was making for her parents and her son going to school in London. At this time, Sergei appeared at the front door and this was good because emotions were running high and because both of them respected him so much, they cooled their heels and greeted him like he was their long lost brother or son.

This night tour of Russia was different than the first in that they would be visiting several of their parks located at higher elevations where all of Moscow would be lit up like the grand old city it was. It was many centuries older than St. Petersburg and those who lived here didn't mind telling you so. The city to its north was nothing more than another piece of swamp land when magnificent structures like St. Basil's Cathedral was celebrating its 100th birthday. In fact, it wasn't too long ago when the celebration of its 450th year of completion in year 1560 took place.

The parks were ostentatious with their musical water fountains, manmade lakes, castles, blending into the Russian forest just 100 yards away. No wonder Empress Elizabeth spent so much of her time in these highlands when she visited Moscow as a young girl. She was a "tom boy" in every meaning of the term often spending time here with Peter 2 who was younger than her. The night with Sergei was ending and what a splendid evening it was. No matter the future, he would never forget this night with Sergei and Olga.

When they got back to the hotel Olga turned back to her business like mode reminding Bill they would need to meet at 7:30am for the breakfast buffet because she wanted to be at the Pragskaya Metro

Station at 8:40am sharp. He thought it was a little strange for her to be so precise but remembering when she set up her beach umbrella (transponder) at Chincoteague this was not unusual.

Nevertheless, Bill was anxious to walk down Old Arabat Street with its interesting array of street vendors, shops, musicians and artists and then from there down to Red Square. An early start would suit him just fine because there were so many interesting places to see and visit and he would be looking forward to having lunch at the outdoor café where Anton, the night bartender had recommended.

Betrayal at the Arabat Metro Station

The next morning came quickly and Olga seemed subdued as they had their morning breakfast together. Bill didn't know whether it was still the anger from his concocted revelation that he had taken the Sapsan to St. Petersburg to make love to Vera in the very room and bed she had stayed in while there or perhaps she had new thoughts on her mind. He was wondering if he should tell her that the trip to St. Petersburg was nothing more than a fantasy trip but after her overreaction, he decided to let that dead dog lay rather than stir up more emotions. They started their walk to Pragskaya at 8:25am and arrived at the platform at 8:35 and it would be just a minute wait for the 8:40 metro train. From there, they counted the seven succeeding stops before they would arrive at the old Arabat Station where they would get off and take the next metro to Red Square.

When the train arrived, it was packed like sardines with morning Muscovites going to work, and there was absolutely no way to get one more person on. But inexplicably, Olga threw herself on and as the door slammed on his face she was waving goodbye through the glass door as if it would be a final goodbye.

As Bill stood there stranded on the platform, he would never forget her face as she looked back… one of deep concern and anguish, and somehow he sensed that his day would not go as planned. Being unfamiliar with the Moscow Metro System, he decided to take the stairs and escalator to street level and as he walked up the street he recognized some of the structures from the earlier trip downtown several days ago.

He walked over to Old Arabat Street near the bench where Olga had marked on a map where the taxi would be located in the city in case either got lost. He assumed Olga would take the metro to Red Square and would meet him there.

As he walked down Old Arabat Street past the vendors and musicians and, yes, an American style McDonalds, there was a taxi waiting near the end. Not understanding very much English, it was easy for the cabbie to understand the words Red Square and GUM. He interpreted it to mean Bill wanted to be left off at the GUM shopping plaza which was the structure on the opposite side of the Kremlin with the parade grounds between them. When he got there, he walked to the cobblestone parade grounds for 30 minutes looking for Olga.

She was not answering her cell phone; each time Bill got a recording that the number being called was no longer valid. Not knowing what to do, he decided to join an English touring group going into St. Basil's Cathedral. It was spectacular beyond description and when leaving, he was approached by three uniformed armed officers with the letters RIS emblazoned on their jackets. They asked to see his passport and visa and then asked if he was Bill Bond at which time he nodded his head yes, saying "da" at the same time. "In this case you need to come with us to RIS headquarters."

House Arrest in Chelyabinsk

Almost immediately, Bill understood that this detainment had something to do with Olga's behavior when she left him stranded at the Old Arabat metro station. He could not help but to wonder whether his plight would be similar to that of Mikhail but surely in this day of enlightenment they wouldn't dare to do something that radical to a USA citizen and what would their possible motive be. Maybe they were able to intercept the e-mail that Irina Koslovovich had sent to him but the security system he had purchased was impenetrable if you were to believe the company who sold it to him.

When they arrived at RIS headquarters, he was immediately whisked onto an elevator that took him down beneath street level what seemed like at least 15 floors. It reminded Bill of the coal mine elevator he rode down as a teenager in Western Pennsylvania that convinced him he didn't want to be a miner. When he thought of these brave men willing to go down that shaft to bring affordable electricity to American homes and industry, he had little love or respect for those elite greenies that have nothing but disdain for those miners and are more than happy to kill a vital industry.

But that is another story for another time because right now Bill was in Russia and maybe 150 feet beneath the streets of Moscow, being led down a dark makeshift hallway and now into a room with very little lighting. He was asked to sit at a table with two chairs. Two of the agents left the room while one remained at the door, when a lady with a dull gray uniform and a hair style reminiscent of the Soviet days entered the room to take the other chair.

"Good afternoon Mr. Bond, we meet again but this time under completely different circumstances." Her face was unmistakable, as beautiful as ever but somehow she looked plain. The low cut blue dress was missing, the smile was gone, the Betty Grable legs were hidden under that ugly uniform and her voice was stern and unfriendly. This was the other Dasha Brumel. She then turned on the lamp sitting on the table, opened up her briefcase and took out some photographs.

"Do you recognize the man in these pictures, Mr. Bond?" How could he not?

They were taken on the beach at Chincoteague before he suspected that Olga was a spy. Her words were coming back to him, "Stand right here Bill and place your hands here" and as he perused the two dozen or so pictures those viewing them would get the impression that he was her accomplice. Olga's grand plan and scheme was brilliantly conceived and masterfully implemented. He understood that CIA agents at Langley also had these pictures and he was a marked man, a traitor. He was now a man without a country.

He would no doubt be used as trade bait except, he would be judged more harshly than a spy. Death is usually the punishment for traitors. His fingerprints were all over that beach umbrella and those Frisbees and who knows what she did with them. Their near death experience at Chincoteague should have been a bond between them that was permanent and unbreakable but in the end it meant nothing to her.

As he sat there in the chair looking at the pictures, he wondered what would happen to him now. He was about to find out as Ms. Brumel was about to lay out his future over a time period which she could not predict.

She explained that the CIA was holding Max Boutay who at one time was a high-ranking agent in the RIS who became a turncoat handing over highly classified documents regarding their spy in the sky program to American authorities and Russia wanted him back. Bill, just wanting to flirt with the ladies to make his retirement more interesting was now being perceived as another Benedict Arnold within the country of his birth that he loved so much?

Ms. Brumel seemed to have softened somewhat as she began to lay out his itinerary over the foreseeable future. "When you leave this room, you will be taken to the fifth floor where you will undergo a medical procedure to implant a micro-chip in your chest so we can track your location around the clock. Remember our surgeons are highly skilled doing this very minor operation but since the incision is close to the heart, any attempt to remove it by others than those trained by us could result in your untimely death."

With that, she shook his hand and turned him over to her three associates who then escorted him to the fifth floor where he was introduced to the surgeon who would place the micro-chip in his chest. "Hello, my name is Dr. Vladimir Sementsova, I will be giving you a localized sedative and I promise to have you back on your feet in no more than two hours."

Of course, Bill had no choice in the matter and when he came out of his slumber, he was taken to a small dining area where he had some steak and eggs. From there, he was escorted to what would be his quarters at least until the following morning. He was still groggy from the sedative and after his grueling day, he needed some sleep and he must have gone out like a light because the morning arrived quickly. He noticed what appeared to be an overnight bag near his bed with his name on it. When he opened it, there was underwear, a couple of shirts and some toiletries and that could only mean he would not be able to go back to his room at the Katerina Park Hotel.

Soon an associate knocked on his door and informed him that after breakfast he would be going on a multi- hour journey. All his personal belongings at the hotel had been confiscated and would be placed in storage and it included his computer. After breakfast, he was led out to a specially equipped van and it was then he was told he would be going to Chelyabinsk where he would be officially placed under house arrest.

Polina Botkina

His caretaker in Chelyabinsk would be a young RIS operative by the name of Polina Botkina. The accommodations in the van were quite comfortable and the journey would give him more time to think which was both good and bad. Not being able to communicate with his loved ones was his greatest concern. He was happy he was able to get some funds to Vera but what would she think if too much time passed by without hearing from him?

The trip to Chelyabinsk was well thought out. About every six hours, they would stop at a place previously chosen to get a bite to eat and freshen up. When they got within several hours of Chelyabinsk, they stopped at a military style clothing store where Bill was allowed to shop for trousers and other items, compliments of the state.

They were now on the outskirts of Chelyabinsk and then he remembered that this was the city where Lavrent Beria ordered chemists to develop the poison ciyanara (aka sayonara) that killed Mikhail some 70 years after it had been perfected. It was a deadly poison for sure but one flaw in the development process was that traces of it in the human tissue could be detected many months after it had been administered.

His mind would rush from one thought to another remembering how his good friends tried to dissuade him from going to Russia to be with Olga because they believed she was up to no good. At the time, it angered him that they felt that way about a woman he cared so much about. How right they were.

Less than three weeks ago, he arrived at Domodedova Airport with great expectations and now he was to be used for trade bait for their former master spy Max Boutay. This beautiful woman who looked so radiant and sexy as she stood there at the airport waiting for him to clear customs had a plan for him which she executed with the skill and cunning of a seasoned spy with many years of experience.

He wanted so badly to visit Russia not only to be with Olga but to fulfill a dream that he had for over six decades. He would never forget sitting at his desk in the fourth grade of elementary school pondering the map of this giant land Russia and wishing he could visit there. But of course he was too young and poor in those days and besides those was the years of Soviet control and Stalin was the head ringmaster.

Now they were pulling into the long and winding driveway on the property where he would be staying for an undetermined amount of time. The house was barely visible because it was constructed with lumber from the huge trees that were so prominent on this piece of real estate. He would later learn that it was the summer home of Joseph Stalin's mistress Alyesa Ivanova. This was the perfect venue for having an affair because it was built in such a way to provide the occupants complete privacy from the outside world.

As they walked to the entry door, they were met by a pretty petite woman who looked to be about 25 and she introduced herself as Polina Botkina. She would be his personal guard and interpreter during his stay in Chelyabinsk. It didn't take long for her to lay down the ground rules in what she expected from him both here in the house and outside it. She reminded him that a micro-chip was implanted in his chest and should be a constant reminder that he was under 24 hour surveillance by the RIS who knew his exact location within a half block area. And if he ever wondered beyond the city limits of Chelyabinsk, their trained dogs would be released to hunt him down and his very survival would be in doubt.

"We will be provided a cook and housekeeper for two hours three days a week and during those hours, you will have no contact with them. They will arrive at 11am and leave at 1pm every Monday, Wednesday and Friday. During this time you will go to the small house on the back edge of the property 30 minutes before their arrival. You will be provided current magazines that are popular with American men so boredom should not be a problem for that short amount of time."

She continued on by explaining there would be ample opportunities for recreational activities. "During these outings, if anyone should ask personal questions just tell them you are a guest of Vladimir Putin and they will know not to take it any further. Your bedroom and bath will be on the second floor and mine will be on the east wing of the first floor. You will address me as Ms. Botkina and you will be Mr. Bond at least for now."

"Later, if everything goes well, we can use our first names at non-formal venues. The state will provide ample funds for recreational activities and personal needs such as bathroom supplies, etc. By this time, you should be very tired after such a long journey so maybe a nap would be something to consider. There are always ingredients in the refrigerator to make a sandwich as well as fruit and pastries in the kitchen pantry. In the west wing there are television sets as well as approved video's and movies in English so you are welcome to go there any time in the day or evening. Although television programming will be in the Russian language, English subtitles are available by pushing the CE button on the remote. Also, there is an exercise room in the basement with modern equipment. Finally, any attempt to suggest having any kind of sexual contact will be dealt with appropriately. Well Mr. Bond, I believe I have covered all the essentials for now. After your nap, I will be in the west wing watching a movie titled, Rear Window, at 9p.m, and you are welcome to join me if you so choose. I am a big Alfred Hitchcock and Jimmy Stewart fan."

At this time, Bill agreed they were also two of his favorites and would be looking forward to this evening to join her. When he walked up the steps to his room, it was anything but austere with a king sized bed and a shower head that was affixed to the wall instead of the hand-held variety at the hotels he stayed at in Moscow, St. Petersburg and Kostroma.

It was now late afternoon and when he lay down for his nap, he set the clock provided to 8pm to be sure not to miss the 9pm movie with

Ms. Botkina. Like the other Russian ladies he had come to know, she had a personality that any guy would find difficult to resist. She was petite but it was easy to see that all her body parts were well constructed and developed. There was little doubt she was a fitness nut. Her dark hair, piercing green eyes and sharp mind combined to make her a very attractive woman. She was the classical example of "you can look but dare not touch" type he had heard and read about over the years.

Of course, Vera Petrova was his love and to think of Ms. Botkina in any sexual way would be disrespectful to Vera. For sexual relief, he would go to his bedroom or shower and think of only Vera. When he arrived at the west wing recreation room, Ms.Botkina was sitting there wearing bright red pajamas that didn't seem to fit her conservative personality but he thought it was her way of creating a more festive and relaxing atmosphere.

"Good evening Mr. Bond, you are very punctual. It is exactly 9 o'clock and I will start the movie. There are cookies, popcorn and soda on the serving table so help yourself. You can sit in the lounge chair over there where the view will be good."

He thanked her for her hospitality and although he wanted to kiss her hand to show appreciation, he decided that just words would be better for now. The movie, Rear Window, was about a man (Jimmy Stewart) who was confined to his small Brooklyn apartment with a broken leg in a cast. Most apartments in those days did not have air conditioning so windows would be open to get fresh air and of course the noises and activities of surrounding units were easy to see and hear. Jimmy witnesses a murder in a unit across the courtyard and convinces his visiting girlfriend (Grace Kelly) to become involved to foil the murderer (Raymond Burr) from moving the deceased body from his apartment.

The movie includes other subplots that are taking place in other apartments in the complex and it becomes a real thriller. When it ended, both Polina and Bill stood up and clapped showing their appreciation for a very entertaining movie with great acting by all and for sure it was a real Alfred Hitchcock masterpiece. When the night was over and the days and weeks went by they must have watched all the Hitchcock movies at least twice.

After several months had passed, Ms. Botkina finally gave permission to call each other by their first names. Sometime later both began to discuss some things about their personal lives and she opened up about her deceased husband. She had met Alexander at an RIS training facility just east of Moscow. They recognized early that they had an intellectual and physical attraction for each other and married just one week after graduation.

On their second anniversary, they decided to join a festive group who were taking a cruise on the Moscow River when their boat plowed into the back of a coal barge throwing those in the front of the boat into the water, killing seven of the 20 passengers on board. Alex was one of the seven and although Polina didn't sustain any serious body injuries, the mental scarring could never be erased. To deal with her sorrow and anguish, she took a four week medical leave to ascertain if she wanted to continue to pursue her career in the RIS. It was such a traumatic experience she wondered if she could perform her duties with the diligence and mental alertness expected of her. Her rigorous training on how to deal with adversity and near death situations served her well during her two fortnights off.

During that period Polina spent much of her time in the small village just northwest of Moscow where she grew up visiting her parents and grandma. She would go to a small cathedral everyday with her mum and she entertained the thought of becoming a nun. Most of the young people had gone to the big cities to secure jobs and unless you were a farmer or could secure a job at the local wheel bearing factory, there was little hope for gainful employment.

And for educated women like herself, the choices were slim and none in any rural area or small town. But while there, her mind began to heal and she decided to continue her career in the RIS. Upon her return to duty, she was assigned to the Moscow office where she was introduced to her new boss Dasha Brumel. It happened to be in the same time frame that Ms. Brumel had come back from St. Petersburg after conducting her interview with Bill Bond. Little did he know at that time that his fate was sealed. Polina Botkina was given all the details as to what her assignment would be.

It was a moving story and Bill wanted to hold her in his arms to console her but he knew it would be improper even if she were to allow him this small gesture of concern. Any move that could lead to some form of passion would be a violation of her rules. Months had passed since he arrived in Chelyabinsk and their respect for each other was gaining momentum. Bill had taken dancing lessons for many years and now and then she would put on a CD from her collection and ask him to show her some steps in various ballroom dances like the waltz, foxtrot and tango which he was more than happy to do. Although the tango would bring their bodies close in a sensual way, their respect for her deceased husband and his devotion to Vera never allowed their emotions to take them from the dance floor to the bedroom.

They were now doing their daily workouts together in the basement exercise room. Bill would end his routine about ten minutes before Polina but always remained there until she had completed her more stringent block of weight lifting exercises. When they both sat down to rest, they were amazed when they looked at the basement oak wood joists that were still in excellent condition after 90 years.

The house was built in 1920 and in 1928 Joseph Stalin purchased it for his 19 year old mistress Alyesa Ivanova although he was still married to Nadezhda Allilueva. Stalin had moved his famous tank factory to Chelyabinsk to protect it from any possible German attack since Adolph Hitler was becoming a growing menace at the time. Stalin did not like to fly but he loved trains and it was said he could sleep as long as 14 hours on a moving train. So a special locomotive, sleep car and service car was built just for his trips to Chelyabinsk where he would inspect his tank factory and chemical laboratories during the day and be with Alyesa in the evening here. He would call these eight day excursions his working holiday.

In 1928, Alyesa was called in by the Kremlin staff to help with a party Stalin was having for the French Ambassador's wife. While carrying a tray with glasses of French wine, Stalin called her over to his location while he was talking to the Ambassador and while taking one to give to his guest, Alyesa's co-workers noticed he had an eye for her and two days later he summoned her to the Kremlin where he seduced her and told her of the arrangement he made for her at Chelyabinsk.

After Stalin passed away in 1953, Alyesa wrote her memoir describing her life with Stalin over a 25 year period and about the seduction that night in 1928 and her subsequent affairs when he would visit Chelyabinsk. Stalin's heirs hunted down every copy of that memoir and destroyed them and threatened any publisher who tried to print it. When Stalin died Alyesa was just 44 and she lived in her house until 1960 when she sold it to the State for a tidy sum. She had married a chef who worked at a restaurant she frequented often and they eventually moved to Moscow where they opened a very successful café. Alyesa passed away in 1999 at age 90.

Needless to say, Bill was fascinated with this most interesting part of Stalin's life since you would read nothing like this in the text books of the era.

Tomorrow, Polina would leave for a two week vacation and just like one other time she took her vacation, an elderly RIS agent would take her place and her strict rules really frustrated him. For God's sake, Bill was an old man and he had to retire to his bedroom by 9:30pm. If he wanted to watch a movie it would have to end by 9 which was the starting time when Polina was here. Bill had been here for 9 months and was not able to communicate with Vera. At least with Polina, he had an attractive young woman in the house and his loneliness would not be as severe.

The Sensual Bolero

During Polina's absence, Bill would spend extra hours in the basement exercise room and every time he would punch the heavy punching bag he pretended it was the old hag upstairs. Of course, it was unfair of him to feel that way about her since she was just doing her job. The two weeks went by slowly but at least Polina would be back tomorrow so it was something he could look forward to. When he awoke the next morning, he was feeling buoyant because Polina would be here in a few hours. When she arrived that afternoon, she seemed to be just as happy to see him as he was to see her. In fact, after her replacement went out the door, they hugged and she gave him a kiss on the lips which was a first. She seemed excited like she wanted to say something important when all of a sudden,

"Bill you are a great tango dancer, can you do the bolero?" Bill was wondering what she had up her sleeve so to speak.

"Yes, I love the bolero; in fact, it is one of my favorite dances." At which time she took him by the hand and led him to the recreation area at the west wing. "Help me move the furniture out of the way." Now he was beginning to see what she was up to. She had created enough open space to do a nice bolero. She had brought in a shopping bag and took out a white silk shirt and tossed it to him. "I bought this for you; please wear it for me."

Up to now, he had been wearing shirts issued to him by the RIS. As he took it off and put the new one on it was similar to the ones they used in dance competition. "Oh Bill, you look so handsome, please stand right here, I will be back in ten minutes." At this time, she picked up her shopping bag and scurried toward the east wing where her bedroom was located.

About five minutes into his waiting, Bill began to hear the sound of bolero music. Of course, he recognized it as Maurice Ravel's version of the bolero and then a door opened that he didn't know was there and Polina began to move toward him in staccato like steps and he hardly recognized her. The dance dress of fire red with slits showing her inner thighs and matching red underpants and strands of black hair over her eyes, she was as stunning as any woman he had ever seen, and now she was within an arm's length of him. Bill pulled her close to him and he got a good view of her breasts that she had never permitted before. Every move he made she countered with a sensual response and soon the circulation of blood in his body had its effect. She smiled as if to say it is okay Bill and then she moved her torso against him and within minutes, he achieved a full release.

The 17 minute version of Ravel's bolero ended almost at the same time, at which point she led him over to a lounge chair where he sat down, sweating profusely. Within minutes, he was asleep and all he could remember her saying was "Thank you Bill, you helped me fulfill a dream." About three hours passed before he came out of his slumber because the clock on the wall read 8pm and Polina was not around. He understood he had to go upstairs and take a shower after his mini-explosion a few hours earlier.

It was apparent that Polina had taken dance lessons while on her two week vacation. She was a natural and Bill was a little embarrassed because never before had this kind of event occurred in all the years of dancing with some really sexy women. She had warned him early that there would be no sexual activity between them and they both adhered to her admonishment in good faith. But he had never done the 17 minute version of Ravel's bolero and he was surprised he had the stamina to complete it before practically collapsing.

As he sauntered upstairs to his room and into the shower, he assumed that Polina was resting because it was the first day back from her two week vacation and after her performance, she had to be exhausted. After his shower, he went downstairs to the kitchen and made himself two poached eggs and a piece of toast with a glass of orange juice.

Later, Polina appeared in her night robe and kissed Bill on the forehead and thanked him for everything and then, "Your anatomical reaction was very natural and neither of us should feel guilty for what occurred. I made it happen by pressing my torso against you so let's forget it and now why don't you make me a poached egg and piece of toast and since we are both tired, we can retire after we have satisfied our appetites." He didn't know if she would extend him an invitation to be with her and he was hoping it would be a decision he would not have to make because of Vera.

When they finished their eggs and toast, they retired to their separate bedrooms and although he had taken a nap after their bolero he was more than ready to retire for the evening. Over the next several months they decided to never repeat another bolero. It was like taking a memorable cruise where you meet new friends and have a great time but trying to do it again can rarely be duplicated.

Bill was now in his 13th month at Chelyabinsk and Polina was now on her third two week vacation and each time it was getting more difficult to deal with her replacement lady because of her unreasonable demands. He was not a child and didn't appreciate being treated like one. Then on the ninth day of her normal 14 day vacation, Polina returned early to Chelyabinsk and immediately released her replacement and Bill could sense that some serious event was the reason she had come back early.

"Bill you are now free to go back home to the USA."

Polina could tell from his reaction that he was having a difficult time digesting the news. His thoughts were running in all directions. Had he been traded for Max Boutay and would he be tried for treason when he returned to the USA?

"I know what you are thinking Bill but there was no trade. Olga Kornakova surrendered to American authorities and convinced them you had no part in her espionage activities. You are a free man."

As they looked at each other, tears began to appear in both their eyes and they embraced in such a way as if to say we are going to miss each other but both understood the implications of his freedom were far more than either could comprehend at this particular moment. "Go up to your room and get yourself together emotionally and I will meet you in the west wing recreation room at 6pm and will explain everything to you at that time. Bill was feeling dizzy from the emotions that had overtaken him and he definitely felt the need to lie down and gather his thoughts.

From Chelyabinsk to Moscow

Bill's first concern was Vera Petrova. She had not heard from him in nearly 14 months and heaven only knew what she was thinking. He was feeling so much better about Olga but her involvement in the demise of Mikhail was still heavy on his mind. It was now close to 6 p.m and as he walked down the steps to the recreation room, he was still feeling the aftershocks from the news he had received four hours ago.

Polina, in her usual thoughtful but now subdued manner, asked him to sit down and she would explain as much as possible the turn of events that gave him his freedom. She explained that on her recent two week vacation, she was notified to report to RIS Headquarters in Moscow before returning to Chelyabinsk. When she arrived there, Dasha Brumel handed her this transcript and asked her to deliver it to Bill promptly. "Take it and read it and it will be better than me trying to explain it."

"It was learned by our Agency that sometime during the past month Olga Kornakova turned herself in to the American Embassy in Moscow and admitted that while working in the USA at a place called Hannah's on the Delmarva Peninsula, she was engaged in clandestine activities for the RIS. During her visits to Chincoteague Island to set up her spying equipment on the beach, she enticed Bill Bond to accompany her where she encouraged him to pose for photographs making it appear as if he was assisting her. She had now convinced American authorities that he was unaware of her espionage tactics. Therefore, he no longer had any value to our side and by order of Vladimir Putin, he was to be released immediately.}

WOW!!! That was the extent of the transcript but it still left so many questions unanswered at which time Polina said she would try to fill in the blanks. The most obvious question was where is Olga now?

"Our Agency was able to ascertain that agents working within the American Embassy were able to get her across the border into the Ukraine where a special aircraft was waiting at a secret airport near Kiev where they flew her to London. From there, she boarded a CIA plane that took her to Dulles Airport in Washington and then onto CIA headquarters at Langley, Virginia." This was an unbelievable turn of events and the fact that Putin had ordered his release made it seem it had been turned into an international event of some importance.

But now, it was time for Polina to explain how his impending release would be handled regarding time and transportation. "You will depart here at 7:00 in the morning at which time I will drive you to the train depot and secure rail tickets for you. I have permission to withdraw thirty thousand rubles from a designated account which will be ample funds for any expenses pertaining to food, fees and allowances that may be charged by others during your trip.

"When you arrive in Moscow, a car will be there at the train depot to transport you to RIS headquarters where you will get your final instructions and of course you will have the micro-chip removed from your chest."

With this, she stood up and told him he needed to rest because it would be at least a 30 hour journey to Moscow. Bill entered a little bit of levity at this time by asking if he could keep the shirt she gave him when they did their Ravel bolero. She laughed and said of course and they embraced before he went up the stairs to his bedroom for the last time.

The ride to the train depot the next day was an emotional one. Polina extended her right hand and took Bill`s left as a gesture of respect and friendship. They had lived together for nearly 14 months and they watched scores of movies in the west wing, exercised together, went on tours of the city, danced together and neither would ever forget their Ravel bolero. He wondered what her next assignment would be but decided not to ask.

Polina stopped at the bank on the way and handed Bill the 30 thousand rubles in a brown envelope and when they arrived at the train depot she secured his tickets and now in 20 minutes he would board for the long trip to Moscow. When she handed him the tickets out on the platform, they embraced tightly and when the last boarding call was made, it was apparent that the tears had been flowing as both of their faces were showing emotions because they would probably never see each other again.

As the train pulled away she was still on the platform as Bill looked out the window of his cabin she was waving and blowing him kisses and he reciprocated. She had reserved the entire cabin for him and although he loved the Russian people he was happy to have the privacy because he had much on his mind. His first thoughts were of Vera Petrova and Olga Kornakova. He was wondering whether his computer was still in storage at the RIS in Moscow and if he would be able to send an e-mail to Vera when he arrived.

The train had now cleared the city and as he gazed out the window, he was getting a look of the real Russia… forests, swamps, villages and fields of barley, corn and wheat and he loved every passing acre. It had been over 20 months since Olga first came to their table at Hannah's. She had performed the job she had been trained to do almost flawlessly. She had used her beauty and guile to lure him to Chincoteague and he was more than happy to be in her company.

After all, he was an old guy who was advised to "flirt with the ladies if you want to have a more interesting retirement." She was 24 years old at the time and she was the whole package. But why did she risk her career and even her life to free him? Maybe she thought back to the day of the big storm when both expended every ounce of their energy to make it to the high ground near the venerable old lighthouse at Chincoteague. They had saved each other from near certain death and in appreciation she had given him her body. On her last night in the USA, she hinted strongly that if he visited her in Russia they would have similar experiences and he began to plan his visit almost immediately and considered himself to be the luckiest old guy in the USA. When he landed at Domodedova, she was waiting for him and she was more beautiful than he had ever remembered. Not long after he learned that there was an Anthony in her life and then their fateful train ride that took the life of Mikhail Popovich.

The woman he loved so much was now on the verge of a total betrayal when she left him stranded on the platform at the Old Arabat metro station. And now here he was on a train from Chelyabinsk to Moscow which was the first leg that would take him back home to the USA while she was languishing in some lonely venue at Langley, Virginia awaiting her fate.

He had a thousand questions he would love to ask her but would he ever get that opportunity? They were now approaching the city of Kazan so the time was going by quickly. The train steward had come by to say they would be in Kazan for a 45 minute layover. That was good news because it would give him an opportunity to stretch his legs and maybe find a good place to eat. He ate a few sandwiches from the train concession stand but they were less than adequate in both taste and nutritional value. Jelly sandwiches without the peanut butter were not all that tasty.

As Bill gazed out his cabin window, the eastern sun was peeking over the horizon and the Kazan Kremlin building was in sight just beyond the Kasanka River. While under house arrest, he read about many Russian cities and their history and Kazan was sometimes referred to as the third capital of Russia because of its strategic location. In 1552, Ivan the Terrible sent his army to kill almost all its occupants with the intent of wiping out all the vestiges of Muslim influence and after the purge he declared it a Christian city.

Today it is a city of over a million people and it was apparent as Bill stepped from the train that Ivan did not accomplish his mission because a healthy mixture of Muslims, Christians and the non-affiliated were prominent within the population. The cool fresh air was invigorating and as he walked the area close to the station, it didn't take ten minutes before he was approached by a "lady of the night." Bill explained his time was limited but he took a five thousand ruble note from his pocket that he had been given by Polina and without warning, she went to her knees and kissed him. With that, he decided to end his walk and pick up a few ham and cheese sandwiches from the station café and go back to his cabin on the train. And now they were on their way and it would be their last stop until arriving in Moscow. The sandwiches and bottle of Nestea had satisfied his appetite and even though it was broad day light and the view out his window was spellbinding, he fell sound asleep.

When he awoke, it seemed as if he had slept around the clock when the train steward came by to say they would be at the Moscow depot in two hours. He would use that time to write letters to Vera, Betsy and a few others so he could have his thoughts already organized when he got his computer back. As he got closer, he was becoming anxious and nervous. Finally, the train was pulling into the depot and when it stopped, he looked out his cabin window there was an athletic looking gentleman in a military style uniform holding a placard with the name Bill Bond on it. When he stepped off the train he pointed to the sign and then to himself as if to say I am Bill Bond. The man introduced himself as an assistant to Dasha Brumel and she was waiting in an official vehicle.

Wow!! For Dasha to actually come to the depot to greet him was totally unexpected and when she motioned to him to sit in the back with her, he didn't know whether to consider it an honor or to fear what she may have had in mind for him.

"Good afternoon Mr. Bond, it has been quite a while since I last saw you. You look good and healthy so Polina must have treated you well." Although in her official uniform, her beauty was apparent, she continued, "I know you will be anxious to get in touch with your loved ones and we will be at our office in about 10 minutes where you can reclaim your computer and I will get you online. You will be taken to the dining room for an early dinner. After dinner, you will be taken to the fifth floor to undergo a minor medical procedure to remove the micro-chip from your chest. You will never know that it was ever implanted, leaving a small mark that will heal completely in a day or so."

"Tomorrow morning, you will board a British plane that will take you to London. At that time, you will be met by an official of the United States Dept. of Justice at which time you will be under their jurisdiction. That is the extent of your debriefing and in two minutes, we will be at our offices and one of my associates will take you to the places I mentioned."

Wow!! She had accomplished the entire debrief on a 20 minute car ride. He knew she was a lady of great skill but this was a remarkable display of efficiency. He was thinking it would be more like a five hour question and answer session. When they pulled into her parking space, she shook his hand and wished him good luck and now she was gone.

Her associate was there waiting and she took him to a room and gave him the computer that had been in storage for 14 months. He was surprised to see it was still in good shape and operating well. His first letter went to Betsy Bond asking her to spread the word that he would be home soon. His letter to Vera Petrova would be more difficult and since he had a two hour time limit for all his messages and letter he would have to be as efficient as Ms. Brumel. He explained to Vera where he had been for the last 14 months but could not give any of the details at this time. He let her know that his love for her had never waned over that period of time. He would have to go back to the United States tomorrow via London where he would write and call her.

The micro-chip procedure went as expected and since he was given a sedative, he slept soundly until morning at which time he heard a loud knock on his door. He was instructed he had one hour to take his shower and have breakfast before departing in their official car to Domodedova Airport. The gentleman taking him was the same one who had picked him up at the train depot yesterday afternoon.

When they crossed over the Moscow River, he could not help but to think of Polina Botkina's husband Alex who had perished in the waters below. Next, they drove through the "tunnel of death" as Olga, Sergei and he had done on their night tours of Moscow some 14 months earlier. Sergei had become his soul brother for sure and paid Bill several compliments by saying he reminded him of his long time mentor and best friend who had passed away a year earlier.

And as they entered the tunnel, Olga would say, "Bye, bye, it was nice to meet you" as if entering the tunnel would doom them all. It was funny at the time but it was only a few days later she left him standing on the metro platform near Arabat Street.

They were now approaching Domodedova and the British Airways flight that he would take was already loading passengers. He was now flying over Kiev and Prague and then to London where an official of the Justice Department was waiting and they boarded a special plane with the letters USA emblazoned on the fuselage. With those letters, any department of the government could make use of the aircraft but today, it belonged to the United States Justice Department. He was briefed on the way to Washington that he would undergo a four hour debrief session by Justice Dept. and CIA officials and if they were satisfied he had no part in Olga Kornakova's espionage activities he would be released immediately with the understanding that they could bring him back if circumstances warranted it.

But in the end, Bill would have to deal with his own conscience. During their final visit to Chincoteague on the day of the big storm, he was almost certain she was involved in some sort of spying venture but after their near death experience and their time at the Quality Inn and all that followed, he convinced himself that he was mistaken about her spying activities.

Surprisingly, when Bill went before the four person panel consisting of two representatives from the FBI and two from the CIA at the J. Edgar Hoover Building in Washington, D.C., they treated him with a degree of civility and respect that he didn't expect. He suspected it was because of his age and the fact that he'd spent 14 months under house arrest in Chelyabinsk so whatever his indiscretion might have been he had already served his time. They wanted to hear when and where he met Olga from beginning to end. He took them through the entire litany from the time he read an article advising retired guys, "If you want to have a more interesting retirement, don't be afraid to flirt with the ladies" to his meeting in London with the FBI. It was a story that seemed to captivate their imagination and the questions that followed seemed sympathetic to his plight.

The one question he had the toughest time with was, "Isn't it true that you were very much in love with this girl and maybe you refused to believe she could be involved in any kind of clandestine behavior?" He thought about it for a while but instead of giving the long answer in his mind, he decided to take the easy way out, "Yes, it is possible that could have happened."

He was now a free man and it was time to drive back to his home in Delmarva. His friends, Jeff and Lisa Scott, had watched over his house while he was detained in Russia, making certain heat was on during the winter and they were kind enough to take his sand-mobile out of his garage where it had been in storage and deliver it to the FBI parking garage the day before.

The three hour drive back gave him time to think about Olga Kornakova and her plight and his future with Vera Petrova. It all seemed surreal as he opened his front door for the first time in over 14 months. Walking through the house after all that time was a poignant moment. It was as if he had never left.

He went to the south sun room and opened up the shades and the back yard, garden, shed and gazebo were still in good condition and he knew his first obligation was to compensate the community fund for making sure his property did not look as if it had been abandoned. It was now time to set up his computer and respond to all those who had sent him e-mails and this would require many hours. During his two hour window at RIS offices in Moscow, he was able to send Vera a short letter to give her a brief account of what had transpired over the 14 months he had been gone.

She responded with this e-mail, "Dear Bill I am so sorry for all you have endured. I love you very much and will be happy to wait until you learn what is possible for you. My tour business is doing very well so I will not need any funds from you. My mum and dad got a nice upward adjustment in their pensions and my son's uncle has come forward to take care of his expenses until he graduates. Except for the fact that I am not with you, my life is okay. Write to me when you can. I miss and love you. Vera"

That letter best describes why he is so fond of her. Yes, their time in the bedroom and shower was very special but it was her unselfishness and honesty he most admired. Her part time job as a "lady of the night" was repugnant to her but she was ready to make any sacrifice necessary to provide support for her parents and son.

As he perused his other messages, he realized how important all his friends were to him. He would try to get back to all of them in good time but he understood that his first mission was to do everything he could for Olga. Yes, he was grateful to her for sacrificing her career to make him free but he still believed that she was the one who slipped the ciyanara into Mikhail's tea on their 17 hour journey from Kostroma to St. Petersburg. What possible explanation could she provide for that? In time, he would know. He understood he could not be completely free as long as Olga was being detained by the CIA.

A Spy Exchange Deal in the Works

Even if Olga was released here she could never return to Russia where the death sentence would almost be certain because now she was the traitor. She had performed her duties effectively as she had been trained using her beauty, charm, and guile to capture Bill's mind and heart. It would be easy for him now to forget she ever entered his life since it was she who initiated the actions that had taken him first to Chincoteague and then to Russia.

But in the end, knowing that he was a victim of her success, her conscience would not allow her to deny him his freedom and the severe punishment he would probably receive if she failed to come forward. Yes, he would love to be in St. Petersburg with Vera but that would have to be on hold for an undetermined amount of time. He could not be completely happy if he allowed Olga to languish in some restricted venue no matter how comfortable, without the freedom to come and go.

However, weeks and months passed and despite his many efforts to visit her at Langley, he could not obtain permission. Every week, he would make the trip to Virginia to ride past the CIA complex just to get the feeling he was close to her and was sharing some of her burden. Yes he had been told that Russian spies were treated well and were given many things to do during their incarceration such as exercise rooms, swimming and even tennis on their outdoor courts to make their lives more tolerable. But throughout history, man's quest to be free was more important than anything else.

But Bill was becoming more frustrated as nearly a year had passed since Olga surrendered herself to authorities at the American Embassy in Moscow. To give him a little piece of mind and deal with his frustrations, he decided to drive to Chincoteague. Yes, his experiences there had covered the gamut with unforgettable memories. But walking its nature trails and being in places where he and Olga had spent so much of their time in the past gave him a feeling of comfort.

He had erased from his mind all the unpleasant things that took place in their relationship. When he arrived there, he went right to the hill near the old lighthouse and getting there on that fateful day saved their lives. He had no clue about Olga's religious beliefs but he could never forget the prayer she delivered that day.

"Dear God, thank you for helping Bill find this safe haven because surely we would have perished without your help."

Now, standing here where they were huddled in his sand-mobile that day, he decided to use the only tool he had remaining since all his previous efforts to see her had failed.

"Dear God, you remember Olga Kornakova well, it was here she gave thanks to you for helping us escape the raging waters from the great storm. She needs your help more than ever now. You know where she now resides so go to her and tell her that her freedom is near."

He could not believe those words were his but it was as if some divine force had taken control of his mind and even his very soul. After going back down the hill, he walked the nature trails for almost two hours enjoying its serenity and there was a peace and calm that came over him that he had never felt before.

On his drive back to Delmarva he felt as if something big was about to unfold and when he arrived home, he went to his computer to write to Vera as he had done twice a week during the year he had come back to the USA. Russia was so much a part of his life now there wasn't a day that would go by without checking out the English version of a site called Russian News and The St. Petersburg Times.

About four days after returning from Chincoteague while spending a few hours searching the internet, he came across an article emanating from a small neighborhood publication in St. Petersburg with bold headlines above the fold, "SPY EXCHANGE DEAL WITH USA IN THE WORKS." At first, Bill thought this was nothing but a cruel hoax perpetrated by some editor trying to get a circulation bounce. All big news stories in Russia come out of one of their major news organizations and there is stiff competition among them to be the first, but yet not one of the majors had one sentence about this.

Nevertheless, he decided to take a few minutes to read the story, more out of curiosity than anything else. The fact that it was publicizing specific time lines seemed to provide some credibility. Also, the neighborhood where the publication was prominent is the same one Vladimir Putin spent the first 18 years of his life, and recently he attended his class reunion in the vicinity of the paper's offices.

Possibly Putin, knowing that a deal was imminent, did the local editor a favor. It was beginning to make more sense and maybe it was possible it had some credibility. If it were true, it would only take a few hours to ascertain its legitimacy.

Some major news outlet on the planet would soon be demanding answers from officials of both countries. About three hours later, the Copenhagen Free Press had picked up the story and they had a sterling reputation for not printing anything without thoroughly checking out their sources. Now it would only be a matter of time before major news outlets in Washington, London, Paris and New York would print something and sure enough the London Times published a special edition giving this story its full attention. Now, the Drudge Report in the USA was featuring the three newspaper accounts. Surely, if all this were true, those promulgating the plan in Washington and Moscow would have to either confirm or deny these reports.

Soon, the foreign office in Moscow alerted the press that they would be making a statement regarding this turn of events at 5:00 Moscow time the next afternoon. The cavernous press room at the foreign office was filling up with cameras and reporters in anticipation. Finally after a full day of waiting a spokeswoman came before the microphone and made this announcement.

"I will not be taking questions after my statement. People above my pay grade will be holding a press conference tomorrow both here and in Washington at 5pm in Moscow and 9am EST in the United States. Now here is what you came to hear. All that you have read in the various publications is true. There will be a very comprehensive exchange of agents and it will be all inclusive. Details pertaining to the exchange will be given to you tomorrow during the dual press conference. This has been in the planning stage for over two years and our goal is to have the full exchange of agents within 30 days. Thank you, that is all I can give for now."

Upon hearing this, Bill's elation could not be constrained. His next job was to ascertain whether Olga would be part of the exchange and if so, would visiting privileges be allowed during the waiting period. In the next several days, he was able to learn there would be a contact person at the CIA who would deal with this issue.

Bill became a real pest at the CIA reception desk, calling every day, and finally he was given the name and telephone number of the contact person. Her name was Mary Heinz. She informed him that visiting privileges would be allowed and she would try to arrange a meeting for him if Olga Kornakova was so inclined.

Olga's Release

Mary Heinz promised to call Bill back before the end of the day. He spent the next few hours in the kitchen close to the phone, making popcorn and eating cookies, anxiously waiting. He was not this nervous since he was under arrest in Moscow and at noon he began to wonder if Ms. Heinz had forgotten him. He understood she was probably inundated with requests so he would need to be patient. Then at 4:50pm, the phone rang and it was her.

"Ms. Kornakova would be happy to meet with you on Wednesday at 10am at the visitor's center." Wow!!! In less than two days he would get to see her, and the anticipation was overwhelming.

For the next 40 hours, he would get little sleep but it wouldn't matter. He spent most of those hours walking the beach and in the James Park nature preserve contemplating all the things he wanted to discuss with Olga. It was now midnight on Tuesday evening and afraid of the heavy traffic in the area of the CIA complex, he decided to get in his sand-mobile and leave now, which would get him to the IHOP Pancake House in Langley about 5am. He would have his breakfast there and then go to the truck stop to get a little shut eye before his 10am meeting. He took two battery alarm clocks to be certain he didn't oversleep. It was about a 15 minute drive from there so at 9am he would leave and now he was sitting in the waiting room at 9:45am. As he sat there, he felt like a teenager who was to meet his girlfriend's parents for the first time.

And then Olga came through the door looking as spectacular as Bill could remember. It was obvious she was taking advantage of the exercise equipment available to her. They hugged and tears streamed from their eyes. It had been nearly 30 months since she left him standing on the platform at the Arabat Metro Station in Moscow. But now he held her in his arms and all that no longer mattered. "Come on Bill, let's walk on the grounds here I am now a trustee so we are allowed to do so."

For the first part of their walk, they talked only of the funny and more pleasant things that occurred during their time together. "From the period of time I first met you until you were placed under house arrest, I was proud of my accomplishments. I was given awards and promotions within the intelligence community where there was both admiration and jealousy. I was sent to the prestigious St. Petersburg branch of the RIS and at 25 years of age only two male 50 year olds were ahead of me in rank. I felt like I had conquered the world. I was given a rent free villa in the nicest part of the city with a car. Anthony came down from Kostroma to visit me from time to time. On his last visit, he asked me if I had given any thought to Bill Bond through this period of adulation. As the days and weeks passed, I began to think a lot about the question he had posed. I was free and happy while this innocent and honorable man who had saved my life at Chincoteague was under house arrest somewhere in Russia."

At this time she began to sob so Bill took her by the hand and led her to a bench and told her not to talk about it anymore since it was water under the bridge and it wasn't worth getting upset over. "No Bill, it is important that I get this off my chest. It has been a never ending nightmare for me and I want to continue. The more I thought what your friends and family were going through not knowing what had happened to you, I began to realize I could never be happy if I didn't do something about it. I had to be patient because regardless of my status, there was always someone watching. Then one day I was assigned to temporary duty in Moscow to follow a person who was arriving on an Iberian Airline flight at Domodedova and was considered a possible threat to commit an act of violence to demonstrate his disgust of the Russian government because they failed to support his organization in their attempt to overthrow the present regime in Spain."

At this time their conversation was interrupted by two men walking their police sniffing dogs toward them who Olga apparently knew and she introduced them to Bill.

When they went on she said they were two agents who had treated her very well in her time here at Langley. "Anyway, when those above my pay grade decided to arrest the possible Spanish provocateur before he cleared customs, I no longer had to follow him as had been originally planned. I was given a few days off to visit Anthony and my parents in Kostroma."

Instead, I decided to stay in Moscow and this would be my opportunity to act. I called Sergei and told him of your plight and what my plan was and he immediately agreed to help me. If there was any chance her plan would work it was crucial they act quickly and decisively. They got in his taxi and he drove right through the gates of the American Embassy where we were detained by the American authorities. I got to some key people there and they immediately agreed to fly me to Kiev and then to Washington via London. The Americans impounded Sergei's taxi but rewarded him later with enough to purchase a new one and then some.

He told the Russian investigators that I had grabbed his steering wheel and turned in to the gates before he had a chance to gain control. He was able to gain his freedom without any punishment. So, Bill, after spending over a year here, I will soon be released. I was told I could stay in the USA for two days after I leave here and I am hoping on one of those days we can be together because there is so much more I want to tell you." At this time, they stopped to get two sodas from the vending machine near the outdoor tennis court. It was notable that she was able to punch in a few numbers without any money or card.

"Now I want to discuss the circumstances surrounding the death of Mikhail Popovich. The woman who prepared the tea during our 17 hour journey was a senior RIS operative I knew only as agent #119. She arranged with railroad security in advance that Mikhail would be in our cabin. Our Agency had irrefutable evidence that he was one of the planners of the terrorist act in January 2011 at Domodeova Airport that killed 40 people and injured hundreds more. You may remember you and I exchanged letters before you came to Russia about this incident and you refused to be intimidated by expressing even a stronger desire to visit our country. Yes, I delivered the tea that led to his demise and I had no regrets then or now because taking innocent lives is a cowardly and deplorable act no matter what your grievance might be with a government policy."

As they began to walk back toward the visitor's center, she wanted to finish the Mikhail episode by saying a third operative actually pushed him onto the tracks after he became disoriented.

"I saw him give you the piece of paper before he departed the cabin but it had no significance since both of your fates had been decided at that time. I didn't recognize him as my instructor at the RIS training facility by appearance alone but his lisp was unmistakable. He got what he deserved and I was proud to have participated in his execution. When Dasha Brumel interviewed you in St. Petersburg, she had no idea how Mikhail had perished. The mission was carried out by the international branch of the RIS and since we have a distinct separation most times, the domestic wing has no idea what we are up to and vice versa. It was designed to work like that by the old Soviet operatives and since it worked well for them there was no reason to change after 1991 when all the other changes in Russia were taking place."

When they got to the door, she again reminded Bill that she wanted to spend one day with him when she was released. She would be allowed to use their computer for one hour a day starting tomorrow and she would e-mail him to arrange everything.

With that, they embraced and now it was time to go to his sand-mobile and head back to Delmarva. It was a wonderful reunion. Her explanation on why Mikhail had to be eliminated erased a lot of negative thoughts in his mind about her. The fact that he was the victim of her spying ventures was understandable since that is what she was trained to do and she accomplished her mission with "flying colors."

But in the end her conscience had emerged as the clear winner. He had to believe their time together on the day of the big storm is what gave her the motivation to free him. After all he was old and how many years did he have remaining anyhow? But in the end she was willing to give up her freedom so he could be free. It was a long ride back to Delmarva so he put a CD into the slot and listened to some of his favorite songs including several he had dedicated to her 30 months earlier, "Have I Told You Lately" by Van Morrison and "Without You" by Harry Nilsson. Of course, these were the days before he met Vera Petrova but as happy as he was feeling, they were still an appropriate reminder of those days they spent together at Chincoteague.

When he arrived back at his home in Delmarva he decided that while waiting to get an e-mail from Olga, he could now begin to do the necessary paperwork to obtain the visa for his trip to St. Petersburg to be with Vera. He had been exonerated of any wrongdoing by both the USA and Russian authorities but getting a license to marry Vera would not be as easy as one might think.

Accident on the Blue Bridge

He would have to attend a week of instructional classes to see if he had the demeanor and wherewithal to take on the responsibility that marriage would require. Young women marrying older men was very common in Russia but he was over three decades older than Vera and he wondered whether he might be required to go through some extra hoops before they would grant him a license.

But he loved her and if she was still willing to marry him, he would do whatever was required to be with her. Now that Olga was getting her freedom, his mission here was complete so he circled a date on the calendar for his departure to Russia. His visa would be for two years but once married, he would have dual citizenship. He would work on getting a responsible renter for his Delmarva home for that two year period but eventually he would have to either extend the rental period or sell it down the road but as the old saying goes, he would cross that bridge when he came to it. When he got back from dinner one evening, he received the e-mail from Olga he had been waiting for. She would be released on Friday morning a week from today at 9am.

She went on to say she had some great news for him but it would have to wait. He had sensed that during his visit there at Langley, she had much more to tell him and now he couldn't wait until next Friday morning. While waiting for the week to go by a lady that worked for a local real estate company knocked at his door saying she had heard that he was looking for a tenant for a two year rental starting six weeks from now. After talking with her for just a few minutes, he knew she was the type of person he wanted, someone who was trustworthy and responsible. Another task had been dealt with and since she was willing to take it furnished, he would not have to worry about what to do with his furniture.

It was now already Thursday morning and Bill decided he would leave this afternoon and rent a room at the Marriott Twin Bridges Hotel in Virginia and by doing it this way he could avoid getting up at 4 a.m in the morning for the four hour drive to Langley. He could get a good night of rest and be ready for his day with Olga.

When he picked her up at 9am sharp, she was strikingly beautiful in her black slacks and red sweater. She had already chosen the day's itinerary by wanting to cross the Bay Bridge to do some shopping at the plaza at the fork of Rt. 50 and Rt. 301. But long before they would arrive there, she had some things she wanted to tell him and she started by explaining how she had disposed of her transponder and transmitters before leaving for Russia back on October 1, 2010.

After their dinner the last night, Olga had gotten up early the next morning and loaded them in her girlfriend's car. She had purchased a shovel and digging hoe that week and she drove to the Assawoman Forest to bury them. She knew it would probably not be a permanent burial but it was enough so she could at least get out of the country. Later, she led CIA agents to that location and surprisingly the equipment was still there although the elements did their work and were of little value to them.

They were now crossing the Bay Bridge and Olga now wanted to know about Vera Petrova. There was not adequate time to discuss his plans in detail, telling her only he would be going to St. Petersburg in a few weeks to marry her.

"You know Bill, when I met her in the lobby of our hotel in St. Petersburg, I was very jealous. That was so selfish of me since I had Anthony in my life and our plans for you were anything but honorable. I want you to know I did not meet my past that day as I had told you. I was at RIS headquarters all day, planning for the time we would be in Moscow. I am glad we were able to do the two night tours of Moscow with Sergei before you were placed under arrest the next day. Our friendship with Sergei proved to be invaluable when he was willing to sacrifice his taxi and maybe even himself to get us through the gates at the American Embassy."

They were now pulling into the parking lot of the shopping plaza and she decided that now was the time to get to the great news she had promised in her e-mail to him.

"Bill, during my stay at the CIA facility I met an agent whom I have become very fond of. He wanted to marry me as soon as possible after my release but I told him about Anthony and that I needed time in Russia before I could be sure. We agreed to wait a year to see if we both felt the same way. Kind of like the way you and Vera were doing although you guys have been separated nearly 30 months. I wish both of you all the happiness in the world."

It was not news he had expected, thinking she would not consider anyone else but Anthony. As a matter of fact, he was under the impression they were living an intimate lifestyle without the marriage vows. "Well Olga you certainly did surprise me and it is going to take me some time to digest everything so why don't you do your shopping and I will use the time to get some walking exercise. Do you need some money?"

She shook her head no saying Ben had lent her his credit card with a generous limit. She showed him the card and the name Ben Stevens was imprinted so now his identity was known. After about an hour of shopping she requested to go to St. Michaels, Maryland next. She remembered a nice pub there when she was staying and working in Delmarva and since both were getting hungry, it was a logical destination.

He had imagined that they would be going back to the Washington area after but that is when she broke some more news. "Ben owns a townhouse in Easton, Maryland and I will be staying the last night and my last day tomorrow with him." The itinerary she had planned was well thought out. Easton was a short distance from St. Michaels and Easton wasn't that far from Delmarva so she was making it easy for Bill.

Their day together was almost over and after having a fried oyster and potato salad early dinner, they took a stroll down the street of the old town reading about some of its history posted on the buildings and homes. It was now time to drive to Easton where he would meet Ben Stevens. Ben had drawn a small map for Olga on how to get there once they reached the city limits. But within a few miles Olga asked Bill to park at a private space before going all the way to his townhouse.

"Bill, do you realize we are sitting in the same sand-mobile we were on the day of the big storm? Please hug me and kiss me as you did that day because we may never have the chance to be together again."

Although he was committed to Vera and her to Ben or Anthony, Bill understood that this was about a special love and respect for each other for all they endured together over the last several years. For the next five minutes, they embraced tightly as only Russian women know how. They are very warm and affectionate and they wear their emotions on their sleeve. They are not afraid to express themselves if they like you. And although some people would think it was scandalous for a woman who was considering marrying a man to have her arms around someone else just a mile or so from his house, Olga and Bill both knew their embrace had an entirely different meaning than sharing a bed on this day.

But now it was time to go that final mile or so and as Olga looked over her map, she directed Bill right to Ben's driveway. Soon, Ben came out and without a doubt he was impressive. He was tall and with a body that resembled a chiseled out piece of timber. Rugged, handsome, and extremely outgoing and friendly he was the epitome of what a woman desired in a man.

"Come on in Bill and have some tea and cookies before you go home. I have heard so many good things about you. I hope you enjoyed your day with Olga."

Bill knew their time together was limited since tomorrow evening she would take an Aeroflot plan to Russia. "Thank you very much Ben but I am afraid I must get home before I melt. I will take a rain check for now but I am sure we will have other opportunities in the future." With that, they shook hands and he waved goodbye to Olga as he backed out of the driveway.

When he arrived home that evening, there was a brown envelop on his door knob that had been delivered by UPS and the contents inside was good news. All his paperwork was in good order and he was now cleared to go to St. Petersburg. His day with Olga was very special but he was looking forward to being with Vera again after all these months. There was still plenty to do to get ready for his return trip to St. Petersburg.

He decided to fly to Moscow first and then take the Sapsan to St. Petersburg. He remembered his first trip on the bullet train 30 months earlier and it was a delightful experience although at the time, he had little knowledge of what was to follow. But none of that mattered now because in less than two weeks, he and Vera would be together again. In their letters to each other, they discussed so many possibilities like building a small house on the outskirts of St. Petersburg and an extension for her parents. It was funny in a way because Bill was older than both of them.

Time was going by quickly and now it was only 48 hours before he would be on a British Airways flight to London and then on to Moscow. It was the same flight he had taken many months before and since he had been treated so well why not give them some more of his business? Vera had written to express how much she was looking forward to the day he would arrive and how she planned this little two person party at The White Cat, Black Cat.

She was going to take some people over to St. Isaacs Cathedral on the morning he would be departing Dulles Airport but after that, her schedule would be free for three days and she was looking forward to spending every minute with him except for the time in the mornings with her parents.

Ben wanted to spend the last night prior to his flight at the Dulles Marriott as he had done on his first trip to Moscow. He decided to send his last e-mail to Vera before retiring for the evening but he got no response but of course it was morning in St. Petersburg and she would be taking care of her parents before making the trip to St. Isaac's Cathedral.

He got up at 4 a.m to take a bathroom break and decided to send her another e-mail since it was now noon in Russia and no doubt she was taking a short lunch break and would be crossing back over the Blue Bridge to pick up the tourists she had left off earlier at St. Isaac's Cathedral. It was a very popular site with a rich history and many times people wanted to be free from their tour guide for a few hours to explore the Cathedral and surrounding area on their own. It was now 5am Eastern Standard Time and 1pm over there and yet no response from Vera. He was now beginning to worry and decided he would not go back to bed but instead he'd take an early morning shower and then to the 6am breakfast buffet.

He called her cell phone which she used infrequently but it was not functioning. He wanted to call the police in St. Petersburg but his Russian was not fluent enough so he just thought since it was about time to get to the airport to check in his baggage he would wait until he got to Heathrow and try again. As he boarded the plane for the first leg, it felt like he was in purgatory not knowing what direction the gods would take him.

The eight hour trip to London was cramped and unpleasant, sitting in the middle seat between two fat guys. He was anything but slim but it was almost as if the airline people who assigned the seats want to punish you for being portly, using the kindest word he could think of. He could afford first class but being the thrifty type, he was always trying to save a buck.

When he arrived at Heathrow he used one of the computers at the terminal but still no word from Vera. The four hour flight to Moscow and the ensuing Sapsan ride to St. Petersburg was a blur. After getting there he took a taxi to the Azimut Hotel where he had stayed the last time. When he walked into the lobby, he went right to the travel desk and sure enough he recognized the agent as one of the ladies who worked there when he was here last time and of all things, she remembered him. After shaking hands and exchanging a few pleasantries, he asked if Vera Petrova had been in the last few days to pick up any tourists.

Her face turned grayish as she began to tell him that Vera's van was involved in a hellish accident on the Blue Bridge near St. Isaac's Cathedral when a beer delivery truck slammed into her. She was the only person in the van at the time, having just left several tourists off at the Cathedral. She is now in the Marinsky Hospital.

Bill didn't want to believe what he was hearing but this would account for her lack of response to his e-mails. At the very time he sent the letter on the night before his flight to London, it was between 8am and 9am in St. Petersburg and she had probably just picked up her guests at one of the hotels.

He reasoned that her condition must be grave; otherwise she would have contacted him by now. He threw his luggage into one of the large storage lockers and took a taxi to the hospital. When he arrived there, he got the worse news he could possibly imagine. She was in a coma on life support and her very survival was in doubt. He explained to the attendant that he had just arrived from the USA and they were to be married in the near future. She asked Bill to follow her but he would only be allowed ten minutes. When he walked over to the bed, Vera looked like a beautiful angel taking a nap, so whatever the extent of her injuries, she was as lovely as he could remember. He placed his right hand in hers.

"Hi Vera I am Bill Bond do you remember me? I am here to nurse you back to health and I will be with you for however long it takes."

She smiled and squeezed his hand but her eyes did not open and she could not speak a word. He kissed her forehead, nose and cheek and no matter what was to follow, they had each other for this moment. And now the tears were flowing profusely and his emotions overcame him to where the attendant took his arm and led him away.

His grief was more than he could bear and when he got into the taxi to take him back to the hotel, the driver handed him some paper towels and although not a word passed between them he recognized his passenger had undergone a very traumatic experience.

When he visited the next day, her brother-in-law was there and he introduced himself with his limited English and they hugged and that is the universal language that everyone can understand. He was the Good Samaritan paying her son's expenses in London and he explained her son had flown in from London hours after the accident to be with her but he sent him right back because he had a bevy of tests this week. Bill agreed that it was the right thing to do because now his future was more important than ever. He also said her ailing parents were being moved to a state-run hospital where all their expenses would be paid by the government. They were not told of her grave condition thinking it better to wait until their caretakers found a more appropriate time.

Their visiting time was ending and Bill sneaked over to give her one more kiss on her nose and cheeks before they were told by the attendant that the hospital administrator had recommended that her life support be removed tomorrow. The doctors had concluded that the injuries were so severe her condition would only worsen in the days ahead. But Bill did not want to believe that all hope was gone, so he returned to the hospital the next day to request that they keep her alive for a while longer and maybe there would be a miracle.

As he walked in, the attendant came over to him and her words were direct and poignant, "Vera has moved on to another place where she will be rewarded for all the good she has done here." And now Vera was gone. She was to be his wife, his lover, his interpreter, his everything.

Life After Vera

Bill went back to the Azimut Hotel and sat down close to the table where they first met. This lady of the night was the most adorable, kindest and responsible human being he had ever met. Bill was in the autumn of his years and he kept repeating to himself, "Why her and not me?" He had never had the pleasure of meeting Vera's parents or son because their love for each other had blossomed so quickly that discussing family on either side was not a high priority. Her stamina and energy level was beyond amazing. After their bedroom sessions, he would be exhausted but she could run a marathon within minutes. It didn't seem like the proper way to think of her now but she possessed so many wonderful qualities and endurance was just one of many.

There would be no formal services and her ashes would be interred at the family plot until both parents had also passed and then all the ashes would be co-mingled and a singular service would be held at that time. This seemed a little odd to him but Russia was changing and old customs were being revised on an almost daily basis so it would not be unusual for close families to adopt this method of burial.

A week had elapsed since he arrived in St. Petersburg and Bill concluded he could not return to the United States. This was Vera's birthplace and her ashes were interred at the Tikhvin Cemetery and here is where he belonged. Besides, he had rented out his house in Delmarva for two years. Also, his visa was good for two years so he would use the rest of the day to try to find a two bedroom flat near the Tikhvin Cemetery. So, he hired a taxi for four hours and it wasn't long before they located a six story building with a sign on the lawn advertising a ground unit flat for lease. The sharp eye of Arno, the driver, spotted it and agreed to go inside with Bill to see if there was anybody available to talk to about the unit.

A young lady came out of a small office to meet them and sure enough, it was a two bedroom flat and it was available immediately. Bill offered to pay for three months in advance if he could sign for and secure a lease today. They went into her office and the deal was made on the spot. Since he still had plenty of time on his four hour hire and the unit was now his, he decided to use some time to look the unit over.

There was a bed and couch and a few more pieces of furniture included in the lease and that is all he would need for now. His move in would be simple since all he had was a few pieces of luggage. The location was excellent with a nice park across the street and within walking distance of the Tikhvin cemetery. In a way it reminded him of Kira and Luba's flat in Kostroma and he wondered if the previous occupants had used it for the same purpose.

He used the remaining 90 minutes of his time to go over to the Azimut Hotel to get his baggage and settle his bill and then return to spend the night here. There were two sets of clean sheets and pillow cases there to start but after a week he would be expected to purchase and maintain his own sheets and blankets and that was fine with him. There were modern washers and dryers in the basement and living on the first floor would make his trips there easy. It wasn't dark yet so he walked the neighborhood to get a feel for what was available since he didn't have a car. There was a small grocery store, a sandwich and pastry shop, and a language school. He would need to stop at all three places tomorrow because he would need some food to put in his small refrigerator but also see what the language school offered so he could go a little further than the 200 words and phrases he had already mastered, although "mastered" would not be an accurate assessment of his skills or lack thereof.

Almost a year had gone by since Vera passed away and twice a week he would go to that hallowed place at the Tikhvin Cemetery where her ashes were interred. It gave him a feeling of comfort that may be inexplicable to some people but he understood it well. He loved his neighborhood and almost everybody that knew him would call him BB.

There were plenty of nice ladies around but his flirting days were over. Oh yes, the first winter was a frigid one and the cold winds coming off the Gulf of Finland made it seem a lot colder than the thermometer was showing. But he had purchased some heavy winter clothing and even on the coldest days, he would walk in the park across the street. Most of the essentials he could get locally but about every month or so he would hire a taxi to take him places. The bus system was good but if he had a load to carry the taxi was best. And then one day he got a big surprise when Olga sent him a letter saying her one year testing period was ending and she decided she was very much in love with Ben Stevens and would be traveling to the United States to discuss everything that had not been nailed down over their many conversations. Bill had almost forgotten she was living in Kostroma for this past year and he didn't think she knew he had been living in St. Petersburg.

He was feeling a little bad for Anthony because he was a real gentleman and could land about any lady he set his sights on but there was only one Olga and she was very special. He remembered Olga always talking about the "man of her dreams" and now she had found him. She didn't mention when she would be getting married or where it would take place but he guessed he would learn more in due time.

It was one year ago that Bill started to take language classes and his assignment for tomorrow would be to read the first four pages of Tolstoy's, War and Peace. He had rehearsed it a hundred times in the privacy of his apartment and he was confident he would do well. He loved the Russian language especially when he would listen to Olga when she would carry on a conversation with Anthony and Sergei.

He was really looking forward to the challenge because after losing Vera, he needed to be with people and his language class provided him that opportunity. After receiving a standing ovation the next day from his classmates for his flawless performance, he decided to celebrate by going on a shopping spree to get some items he had been in need of for a long time. His watch no longer worked and his wallet was falling apart. He wanted to be careful to check every item and card in his old wallet before throwing it and its contents away. Some of people's personal and business cards were over 10 years old.

"It Will Be Therapy We Both Need"

One of the cards was from Dasha Brumel, who had given it to him over three years ago after her interrogation session with him in this very city. She treated him well at the time and how could he ever forget the car ride to the Azimut Hotel with her, Olga, Yuri and himself? Over a year had gone by since Vera's passing and maybe he would call Ms. Brumel just to say hello. It was doubtful her old number was valid but he would give it a try. He had never forgotten that blue dress she was wearing at the time that accentuated all her God given assets.

On several occasions he would begin to push the numbers on his new cell phone but he would always be too nervous continue. He did not indulge in alcohol very often but he kept a bottle of Vodka on hand to relax him enough to deal with these periods when he lacked the confidence to act.

Finally, after a couple shots of vodka, he was able to complete the call. A nice gentleman who was proficient in English answered and identified himself as Ms. Brumel's assistant. Bill explained who he was and he seemed to be familiar with his name. "She is on another line right now but if you will wait a few minutes, I am sure she will want to talk to you." Wow!! He was sure she will want to talk to him and before he could digest this positive sign, "Mr. Bond, it is nice of you to call. How have you been?" Her voice was unmistakable, a sexy, seductive dialect that fit her personality. She had remembered him and gave him a feeling of pure elation. They exchanged a few more greetings and then she asked if it would be okay to call him after work because she wanted to learn as much as possible about his life after his release from house arrest in Chelyabinsk.

When he gave her his cell phone number, she was surprised to learn he was living in St. Petersburg. "I will call you at 7pm this evening." It was now 3:30pm and waiting for her call was like a father waiting for the arrival of his first born. Not that he entertained any hopes of seeing or being with her in person but just speaking to her again boosted his morale after dealing mentally with the memories of Vera who passed 15 months earlier.

The vodka had given him the courage to call but now he needed to walk the neighborhood to clear his mind so he would be coherent and lucid when she called in just over three hours. He went to the pastry shop to have an éclair and hot chocolate and the attendant remarked that she had not seen him in such high spirits. It was late November and the air was frigid and it looked like another severe winter was in store for St. Petersburg. After a long walk, he went back to his flat and removed his heavy clothing and got into his long underwear. He put the kettle on the stove to make some hot tea and now 7p.m. was only fifteen minutes away. He made a final check of his cell phone to be sure it was working properly because this was one call he didn't want to miss.

After drinking his tea, he heard the music from his phone, "Hi Bill, this is Dasha." The fact that she was using first names meant that she wanted their conversation to be informal and it put him at ease. She seemed shocked when she learned he was living in St. Petersburg and being the understanding person she was she did not press him on his reasons for being here. It was not the right time to mention Vera and her dreadful accident.

First, she stated that she was well-aware of the spy exchange program that led to Olga's release and that she had participated in the discussions during the promulgation phase. When Bill told her of Olga's future plan to marry Ben Stevens, you could tell by the sincerity in her voice that she was happy for Olga. She went on to say she would be leaving the Moscow office on Dec. 1 and would be taking a new position as Deputy Commander of the RIS in St. Petersburg on Jan. 1.

Bill was shocked by not only her promotion at such a young age but that she would be coming here to St. Petersburg. This was a very prestigious position and the fact that the appointment had to have the blessing of Vladimir Putin give you some idea about its importance. After all, Putin actually moved through these same circles to attain his position. She went on to say she would have the entire month of December off and was looking forward to getting to St. Petersburg as soon as possible to relax and look over her new house and property that would be provided to her. And then he got the biggest surprise he could ever imagine when she asked him to be her guest at the Stroganoff Steak House on Dec. 10 at 7p.m. She would pick him up in her personal car at 6:40pm. In his state of elation, he asked how she knew where he lived. "I don't, Bill, you need to give me your address now."

He felt so stupid but she laughed understanding that he was having a difficult time digesting her offer. He accepted her invitation without any hesitation and he was in a state of disbelief when they ended their conversation. Was this really happening to him or was he dreaming? It was just a short time ago he was under house arrest in Chelyabinsk by the authority of the Russian government and now he was on the verge of having a private dinner with an important official of that government.

And she would be coming to his modest flat to pick him up in her private car. It was as if all the loneliness he had felt over the past 15 months since Vera's death had disappeared. For sure, he would never get over Vera because what she had given him could never be duplicated. To Bill, Vera was unique not only for her lovemaking skills but for the ability to take on so many responsibilities without complaint or excuse.

But now Dec. 10th was all he wanted to think about and he would use the time between now and then to get ready. The next day, he hired a taxi to take him shopping for dress clothes. He decided on a wool charcoal jacket with matching pants and shirt. He wanted to show her proper respect. Before going back home, he invited Arno, his driver, to have lunch with him at a local deli. When he hired a taxi, it was usually by the hour rather than by the trip so he had plenty of time remaining so not only could he treat the driver but enjoy a meal at a different venue.

While waiting for their orders to be ready, Arno went over to pick up a copy of the St. Petersburg Times. The headline just below the fold read: "Dasha Brumel named RIS Deputy Commander." When he noticed the headline, he never mentioned to Arno that he even knew her let alone that he would be her dinner guest on Dec. 10th. He got to thinking the only possible reason she would be doing this was because she knew he was innocent of any wrongdoing when he was sent to Chelyabinsk and it was her way of saying I am sorry for all you had to endure.

No matter her motive, he was happy that she invited him. Being Deputy Commander of the RIS here is an awesome responsibility. Many think of the Russian Intelligence Service as a "cloak and dagger" organization whose only mission is to spy on western nations and steal their secrets. But their most important mission is to root out and expose the evil elements of international terrorism. The attack at Domodeova Airport in January 2011 that killed and injured hundreds of innocent people was a poignant memory for Bill because one of the masterminds of the heinous act was Mikhail Popovich, the man he shared a four berth cabin with on his trip from Kostroma to St. Petersburg in May of that same year. This incident was a reminder of how difficult their job was because Mikhail Popovich gave the appearance of being one of the nicest people one could know.

Dasha Brumel's achievements were nothing less than spectacular and it took hard work, perseverance, dedication and a sharp mind to get where she was today. She was also not afraid to use her physical assets, her charisma and charm as she had done three years ago when she interviewed him. She also displayed a sense of humor that day on the car ride that annoyed Olga but Bill understood it was all about her competitive nature.

Finally, the day he had been waiting for had arrived. It was an extremely cold day but the skies were clear and the sun over the eastern horizon was spectacular. On a day like today, the monuments and cathedrals here were in their full glory as the beams of the sun sparkled on their bronze and copper rooftops. She would be here at 6:40pm so Bill decided to hire Arno to take him across the Blue Bridge to St. Isaac's Cathedral to spend an hour or so. Yes it was sad to be here in a way because he imagined that Vera had just delivered her passengers in front of this magnificent structure and little did she know that when she crossed back over her life would essentially end in just a blink of an eye. When they crossed back over, he could only cringe when they passed over the very 10 meter area where the beer delivery truck slammed into her van 15 months earlier.

After crossing, they went over to the Tikhvin Cemetery where Bill knelt to say a little prayer to honor the lady he would never forget. When he got to his flat, it was now 5pm and in one hour and 40 minutes, Dasha would be here. To pass the time, he picked up Tolstoy's War and Peace and this time, he would go beyond the first four pages that he had rehearsed a hundred times before his test at the language school.

And now it was 6:30pm and he put on his top coat and walked outside to meet her. It was cold out there and he knew she would insist on punctuality so in case she was a few minutes early, he would be there on a spot that he calculated that would be easier for her to park because he had the utmost respect for this lady that he was growing very fond of. But he didn't have to wait long as her car pulled into the very spot he had envisioned and her passenger window opened, "Jump in Bill, I know it's cold out there."

They hugged and she looked as stunning as he could remember. Dressed in an orange one piece jump suit with a material that resembled the woven braids women do with their hair and there was little doubt this outfit was designed for winter weather. It didn't seem possible that this woman of stature would give him even a minute of her time. On the way over, Bill mentioned he had read the story in the St. Petersburg Times of her appointment and how proud she must be. "Yes, I am proud because it is nice to know that when you spend long lonely hours on a job sometimes practically working around the clock, somebody pays attention. I must tell you I was totally surprised I got the promotion but I feel very confident I cannot only handle the challenge in front of me but also that I will exceed their expectations."

Wow! What a statement to make and it was a good demonstration of her self-confidence. When she said, "exceed their expectations" he assumed that "their" in her phrase referred to Putin and Medvedev. She said she had gone over to the RIS complex yesterday to introduce herself and her framed picture was already in all the offices along with the 55 year old male Commander.

When they went through the revolving doors into this opulent place, he could not help but to think of the time he and Olga were here over 40 months ago when she was dressed in her leopard ensemble. And now to be here with Dasha was more than any man could expect especially considering his age. Two of her colleagues spotted her as soon as they entered and came over to welcome her. Although she probably didn't appreciate that kind of public display, she was the epitome of good manners and grace by shaking their hands and saying she would be looking forward to working with them when she assumed her duties on Jan. 1. The head waiter and host also recognized who she was and sensing that she and her guest needed a little privacy, took them to a table and area where only a few tables were occupied. As they looked over the menu, it was going to take a little while to decide because the choices were so extensive.

While they were trying to decide, the waiter came over with four bottles of wine and Dasha chose a wine from the Sonoma Valley of California called Angeline. Bill was certain she did that to make him feel welcome. After studying the menu, she suggested the combination plate where you would get a sampling of their 12 dishes which included meat, fish, vegetables and fruit. Bill agreed that it was a good choice. It was certainly a delightful dinner and with a piece of Napoleon pastry at the end, it was a feast worth remembering.

It was an evening that he needed badly and he owed it all to Dasha. On the drive back, she insisted on taking Bill over to show him her new quarters before returning to his flat. It was her car and even if he felt uncomfortable, it would be uncouth of him to decline the invitation. She pulled into the long circular driveway and took the parking spot already clearly marked, "Deputy Commander." As she took Bill room to room, the opulence and size of the place seemed extravagant. But this entire city with its magnificent cathedrals and monuments was one of extravagance. It was a mansion more suited to Empress Elizabeth than the Deputy Commander of the RIS. Bill asked Dasha if she would be the only one living here and she told him a driver and housekeeper would take the small cottage in the back on Jan 1. After their tour, she led him to a small cozy room just off the Grand Room. "Take a seat and I will go to the kitchen and prepare a nightcap."

Bill had noticed during the tour the kitchen and the many bathrooms were already stocked with non-perishables. When Dasha returned with the drinks, she had managed to slip into a sexy nightgown and he wondered if he could resist an overture if one presented itself.

She sat down next to him and seemed anxious to tell him that she had married an army officer when she was 18 and he was 30. With his uniform and shiny medals, he was the most handsome man she had ever seen and she was so smitten, she begged him to marry her. It was the biggest mistake of her life and after three years of marriage, they separated because she could no longer endure his many dalliances and drunken behavior. She was a young RIS trainee at the time and decided she would concentrate on her career while trying to forget the three years she had wasted on him.

That was 14 years ago and although she had dated sporadically since then and shared a bed with a few, she had not found any since that had swept her off her feet. "And now Bill, tell me about Vera Petrova." He could not remember if he had mentioned Vera's name to her and since he had just been to the Blue Bridge and Tikhvin Cemetery earlier today, he wasn't anxious to talk about her for fear his emotions would cause him to break down. On the other hand, he had always kept his pent up sorrow inside and maybe this would be his opportunity to share it with someone who might understand the mental pain and anguish he had known for the last 15 months. "But Bill, you need to get it off your chest. Give it a try."

He told her as much as he could about how they had met and how her love of family had captured his heart, but when he got to the part about her accident and her subsequent death, he broke down in a profusion of tears. He was embarrassed because it showed a side of him he didn't want her to see. At this time, she stood up and took his hand and pulled him toward her. "Come with me, at this time we need each other." She then led him to the master bedroom. "You may have noticed earlier that the master bedroom has separate his and hers bathrooms. It was a great idea since women need a much bigger one to keep all their cosmetics, toys and necessities. When I was here the other day, I did peep into the men's and noticed it was pretty well stocked with most of the items you guys require. Of course, being a single woman living alone in Moscow, my apartment had one bath and that was sufficient. Now, take this gift I bought you yesterday and go to the men's bathroom and I will see you in the vicinity of the feathered bed in about thirty minutes. If you arrive before me, get in bed and enjoy its softness. But you better not go to sleep. Do not be embarrassed or ashamed because everything that happens in that bed tonight is therapy we both need."

When he got to the bathroom and opened the gift it was a set of men's silk underwear. He removed his dress clothes and jumped in the shower and turned the faucet to its hottest setting. It was cold outside and the gentle stream of water cleared the scented soap from his now aroused body. He had achieved a full erection and as he dried off and put on his new underwear, he was hoping she would be there when he arrived. It was obvious that this bathroom was meant for men as it had every conceivable item that men would need.

There was an ample supply of condoms and an extension for a penis but Bill wasn't about to take either one to bed with him. If she insisted on him wearing a condom, he could always return. When he got to the bed, there was no sign of Dasha so he pulled away the top sheet and sank into the feathered mattress. He had some wonderful experiences under the sheets with some beautiful women, but never in a feathered bed with a lady of such beauty and stature. Her words, "it is therapy we both need" gave him a feeling of relaxation and he no longer felt guilty of dishonoring the memory of Vera.

Soon, the light began to dim in the room and a rotary style revolving soft light took its place and then she was standing there. She slipped off her night gown and her bikini style panties and bra of purple and white matched the color of the revolving soft light. She had tinted her eyebrows and lips with a purple makeup and this was truly the sexiest woman this side of Mars.

There was no need for handcuffs, rope and chain in her bedroom. She looked at his full erection and smiled as if to say, "For an old guy, you really have something to be proud of." She leaned down to kiss it but then, "no not just yet, there is no need to rush things." and now her body was close to his and all he wanted to do for now was to embrace her tightly because it was nearly 40 months since he last held a woman in his arms this way.

By this time, he had managed to slip off her panties and bra and he began to kiss and caress every part of her body from head to toe. He put his hand on her vulva and her pubic hair was as soft as the feathers underneath them. And then he took his middle finger and massaged her clitoris. She rolled over and whispered in his ear, "now it is my time to enjoy the pleasures of your body" as she moved the tip of her tongue to every part in a teasing way for nearly 10 minutes and then, "what I have done for you is just an appetizer, the entrée and dessert are yet to come."

After dessert, they were both totally exhausted. She left no stone unturned in her efforts to make him happy taking him to places he had never been before. Vera would always be the sweetheart of his life and it is always unfair to compare one woman's performance with another, but Dasha with both her words and lovemaking gave him an unforgettable evening.

And the fact she never insisted that he wear a condom meant that she had confidence in him. Maybe that was the reason she invited him into her bedroom. She knew he didn't have multiple sexual partners and although she had other guys in her bed after her divorce 14 years earlier, he was sure she would select her lovers with great care. When he awoke the next morning, his head was lying between her picture-perfect breasts and his hand was on her inner thigh. She was still asleep and he was still in a state of disbelief because in this city of nearly five million people, he was in bed with someone who ranked in the top five on the political totem pole. When she awoke, she looked at him with a warm smile, "Bill, I can't adequately express how much I enjoyed being with you and we must plan another session before I go back to work on Jan 1."

This was music to his ears because now he would have something to look forward to in this month that was a traditional holiday period in the United States. From the time he was a child, the period between Thanksgiving and New Year's was a time for celebration and reflection. Yes a few would take their good cheer too far, but for the most part, it was a time for joy and happiness. "Now let's take a nice hot shower together and then I am going to make you some breakfast."

The shower together must have been a Russian thing because he remembered both Vera and Svetlani wanted this and for sure it was a stimulating exercise. They soaped each other down and Dasha in her playful way used a touch and feel maneuver that was no doubt designed to get a man fully ready and sensing he was in need of relief, she rinsed him off and went to her knees and in less than a minute, he had achieved a full release.

Dasha looked up and smiled, "Wow Bill that was quick. If I was in the business of doing tricks, it would have been a fast way to earn a quick 3,000 rubles." With that, they completed their rinse and dried each other off. "Now I will fix you that breakfast I promised." Instead of getting dressed in his street clothes, Bill put on the underwear she had bought for him and slipped on a freshly laundered bathrobe that was neatly hanging nearby and went to the kitchen to join her. She was preparing oatmeal and toast and she had not yet put her panties and bra back on, wearing only a white see-through negligee. After his experience in the shower just minutes before, he wondered if he could achieve another hard on. In his younger years, maybe, but at his age, it would be one for the record books. After breakfast and some playful touching, they both got dressed and drove to Bill's flat. And she left him with this thought, "Now Bill, this is the 11th of December and I have 20 days before I go back to work and would like to spend a few of those with you if you are not too busy. I have not spent as much time in St. Petersburg visiting our historical places as I would have liked and I hope you will accompany me. I will e-mail you in a few days suggesting possible dates for you to consider."

Wow!!! Bill thought to himself as he entered his flat. The time he spent with her the past few days was more than he could ever hope for, but the fact she wanted to be with him again gave him a feeling of elation and pure joy. How could this be happening to him? Since he lost Vera, he never thought he could be this happy again. He wanted to lie down on his bed and let it all sink in. In minutes, he was sound asleep and when he awoke hours later his dream was still clear in his mind.

The young Bill Bond was 25 and Dasha was 18 and he proposed to her but she chose a 30 year old army officer instead. While still in his dream, he had dedicated a song to her titled, "A Love so Beautiful" and it was still on his mind when he awoke. It was now 7pm and he had not eaten since his oatmeal and toast breakfast Dasha had prepared for them this morning so he walked down to the deli to have a grilled cheese sandwich and a cup of coffee.

While walking back to his flat, a street vendor had a display of books on a table and Bill purchased Anna Kerenina by Leo Tolstoy. It was a book that was hard to put down and he read it in its entirety before wondering off into dreamland again. He slept in the next day and it was as if he had lost all track of time since his mind was shifting back and forth between the reality of being with Dasha and the 18 year old one in his dream.

Also, the sad demise of Anna Kerenina in Tolstoy's book had reminded him of Mikhail Popovich and the memories were not pleasant. He went to his computer and checked his e-mails and got this message, "Dear Bill, I can't express how much I enjoyed our time together. Is there a possibility I could pick you up at 10am the 16th and be my guest for lunch and an afternoon tour of some of our historical sites? Dasha"

Within a minute, he responded, "There is nothing in this world that would make me happier, With Highest Regards, Bill." He understood he was probably getting this special treatment because of the time he spent in Chelyabinsk under house arrest. Also, maybe she felt sorry for him knowing what happened to Vera Petrova.

When the 16th arrived, it was ice cold and the winds were coming off the Gulf of Finland at a pretty good clip but the roads were cleared of the snow that occurred two days earlier. They spent most of the day at the Admiralty Museum and for any person who loved art it was a place you didn't want to miss when visiting St. Petersburg.

They had lunch at the Stray Dog Cellar and the cabbage soup and stroganoff served with hot Russian style bread was perfect for the winter day. On the 24th and 25th of December, they had a repeat of their earlier "therapy session" and this time their time together was even better than the first because like good students, they both had learned what each other enjoyed most. When she drove Bill back to his flat, she explained she would be taking the Sapsan to Moscow to celebrate the coming year with colleagues.

They agreed to keep in touch by e-mail after Jan.1 when she would assume her new duties. He understood it was possible they would never be together again in a private setting. But she had given him great hope and a reason to go on and he was determined not to let her down.

As the weeks and months passed by Bill got back to doing all the things he was doing before Dasha came back into his life. April was just around the corner and soon the trees and bushes would begin to bloom as they had always done since Peter the Great created this treasured city. Every now and then, Dasha would send him an e-mail but as the months went by, they became shorter and farther apart. He understood that she was very busy but he would never forget those December days and evenings they spent together. Now and then, he would ask Arno to drive by her house when they were out shopping and looking up at the master bedroom window where so much love between them took place gave Bill goose bumps.

The Wedding of Her Dreams

When he arrived home that evening, he received this letter from Olga: "Dear Bill. You may remember some time ago, I wrote you that I accepted Ben Stevens' proposal. Since then, it has taken me more time than I anticipated to get all my ducks in a row in Kostroma and Ben has been more than patient with me for taking so long to set a wedding date. After such a long delay, we decided on July 25th of this year and the venue will be the The Ipatiev Monastery in Kostroma. Consider this letter to be an invitation. I was so sorry to hear about Vera Petrova. If there is someone else in your life now, she is welcome to come with you. I am in Easton now, getting his townhouse ready for his new arrival. He has given me permission to convert one of our five bedrooms into a dressing room and walk-in closet. We plan on having children later and the house is big enough for at least the first two. I think of you often. Love, Olga"

The next day, he received an e-mail from Vadim Matei saying that Olga and Ben had asked him to be best man at their wedding. They could not have made a better choice because Vadim was a real gentleman in every sense of the word. He worked with Olga at Hannah's and like most Eastern European people who came to the USA, he had a second job at Jimmy's Breakfast and Lunch Restaurant on Fenwick Island. That is where Bill met him in September of 2010 and they had been good friends ever since. Although the miles between them were great, they always kept in touch.

Vadim was from Moldova and because of its strategic location, all the other countries in the region as well as the United States promotes good will with their leaders. The distance between Fenwick Island where

Vadim was employed and Easton where Ben Stevens lived was just 90 minutes apart so Ben would drive down on occasion to visit Vadim and subsequently, they became good friends. Olga, of course, was the person who introduced them to each other.

Since their wedding was less than four months away, Bill had to make some plans regarding transportation and hotel reservations. Instead of taking the 17 hour train to Kostroma, he would catch a local Aeroflot flight out of Pulkova to Yaroslavl and then the hydrofoil to Kostroma. Since the wedding was on the 25th, he decided to reserve a room at the Volga Hotel from the 23rd through the 27th which would give him time to visit some places he had grown fond of when he and Olga were there together years earlier.

Meanwhile, his life in St. Petersburg was getting back to normal although Dasha was still on his mind. His daily routine of picking up a copy of the St. Petersburg Times and having breakfast at one of his favorite places was different today. On the front page was a story under the by-line of Svetlani Cheranova concerning the wedding of Olga Kornakova and Ben Stevens in Kostroma. Of course, Svetlani was the mutual friend of both Olga and Bill and had gained the reputation in press circles as not only being first to break big stories, but yet never compromising being first by sacrificing accuracy. But why was this wedding on the front page of a major Russian newspaper? As he read further, the pieces were coming together. There would be 16 CIA agents attending the wedding in honor of their esteemed fellow agent Ben Stevens but after the wedding, they would be joined by 16 operatives of the RIS at the town square in the shadow of the statue of town hero Susanin.

Their joint announcement would be historic. They decided that world terrorism was the greatest threat to all the people on the planet they shared. They were wasting precious resources on clandestine activities against each other, and would instead set up a two country commission to coordinate their efforts against the radical elements of an evil movement that put no value on human life.

Wow!!! This was really big news, and to think that his good friend Svetlani broke the story was especially satisfying to Bill. How could he ever forget the time she extended an invitation to him to come to her cabin in Chincoteague with the words, "And Bill, if you get lonely tonight, I will be here for you."

There was little doubt in his mind that Olga and Ben were her source. That would account for the reason they delayed their wedding, waiting an extra year or so until the details were ironed out. Within days the story was in every newspaper in both countries. The Russian hometown papers of Olga and Svetlani, The Kostroma Gazetta and the Tambov Daily, each carried the story as well.

There was a separate story in the Gazetta regarding Olga, and her gallant sacrifice to free a man from the inequities he had suffered under her watch while working for the RIS. She was also given much credit in influencing her future husband, Ben Stevens, to initiate this historic cooperation between their two countries. Some even referred to her as the female Susanin.

Bill was so proud of all the Russian ladies in his life, because they had achieved so much. Just to know them was an honor he would always cherish.

Summer had arrived in St. Petersburg and the tourists were coming both by ship and plane to enjoy the wonders of this incomparable city. July 23rd had arrived and Arno took him to Pulkova Airport where he boarded a Yak-42 Russian jet for his flight to Yaroslavl. From there, he took the hydrofoil and during his ride to Kostroma, he was fortunate enough to have met a 92 year old Great Patriotic War veteran whose mind was as sharp as anyone 30 years younger. Bill's Russian was proficient enough to listen to some of his accounts of how the Red Army made its final push across Europe to Berlin, which essentially ended the war.

As they looked up the hill from their docking space on the Volga, the Statue of Susanin could be seen. Before Bill debarked, he shook hands with his new friend who would continue on down to the port of Plyos. As he climbed the hills, he sat on the bench about half way up for nostalgic reasons. It was here that he and Olga sat during his visit back in May of 2011. She insisted on going to the small store close by to buy him a Nestea because she knew it had become his favorite non-alcoholic drink during his visit at that time.

Bill had not informed Olga when he would arrive in Kostroma because he understood she had little time for anything other than to get ready for the big day which was just two days away. When he resumed his walk to the top of the hill, there was a taxi waiting with a female driver. She was available to take him to the Volga Hotel and told him she did tours within the Kostroma Oblast. It was his lucky day because tomorrow was his free day and he signed up for two half day tours, one to Ploys and the other to the Romanoff Forest. The cabbie's name was Elizabeth but told Bill he could just call her Princess. When he arrived at the Volga Hotel, the CIA agents who would be participating in this historical event in just two days were checking in. He felt proud to be sharing a building with those who would be participating not only in the event taking place here, but in all of the efforts they would be engaged in the future waging a war against world terrorism… a war they could not afford to lose.

The next day, Princess arrived at 9 a.m and it didn't take long for Bill to learn she was a pure delight. At the Romanoff Forest, they would play "hide and seek" and act like children in the recreation area. She was happily married with two young children but was very generous with her hugs and kisses, which was typical of most Russian women if they really liked you.

Marriage was no barrier when it came to showing their gratitude and affection for others as long as there was an understanding between them that their affection was not an invitation to share a bed. When he got to his room, it was late afternoon and now all his thoughts were on Olga and "the wedding of her dreams" the following day. He received an e-mail from Olga requesting that he sit in the family box with Marina, Andrey and other close family members. This was an honor he didn't expect, hoping to go unnoticed because people in town had read in their newspapers that a man by the name of Bill Bond was the person she risked her career, her freedom and her life for because she knew first hand he did not deserve to be incarcerated on a trumped up charge. In fact, if Bill Bond had not entered into her life, there would be no wedding tomorrow or an important event and ceremony that had attracted the attention of government leaders across the world.

As he lay on his bed, all his thoughts were now on Olga. Tomorrow, she would be the bride and the town would be honoring their new hero. They had been through so many peaks and valleys together but now he wanted only to think of the good times. He removed from his wallet a note she had given him on the evening of September 30th, 2010 before going back to Russia after their memorable summer together.

"My Dear Bill... I wish you all the most positive emotions in the world... the ones you haven't experienced yet... you are a very special and unique person for me... thank you so much for being in my life... Love you, Olga." Of course, these are the kind of words that Russian ladies use in their cards wishing a happy birthday or a joyful holiday but for Bill, it meant more than anyone could ever imagine. Without her in his life, he would not have met Vera, Svetlani, Dasha, and Polina Botkina. Of course, there were so many more including Sergei, Anthony, Marina, Andrey and how could he ever forget Kira and Luba. But tomorrow was Olga's day and he didn't want to miss one minute of it. In the morning, he got dressed in his tailor made suit that the hotel staff had pressed for him on the day he arrived. Princess arrived at the hotel at the appointed time and now it was time for the short trip over to the grounds of the Ipatiev Monastery.

He did not mention to Princess about his past relationship with Olga, instead saying he had received the invitation from the groom whom he had met on a cruise a few years ago. But Princess let him know how proud the town was of their new heroine. She had raised the morale of the entire city and already, officials were talking about a location where a future memorial would be constructed.

As they drove up to the Monastery, Bill could not help but to think of the historical significance of this place. Here is where the Romanoff Dynasty began. Russia had just defeated the Polish Army in a bitter war that had devastated both countries and the ruling committee in Moscow decided they needed someone whose roots went back to the glory days when Ivan the Great ruled.

They determined that a 16 year old boy by the name of Mikhail who was residing at this Monastery was a descendant and asked him to become Tsar and although reluctant at first, he accepted the challenge and in 1613 he became Mikhail 1, the first Tsar and ruled for 35 years. The Romanoffs ruled for over 300 years until the Bolsheviks slaughtered Nicholas 2 and his family in Yekaterinburg in 1917.

But on this day, no one in Kostroma wanted to be reminded of the past because the town hero was about to take the first step in her betrothal to American Ben Stevens. When Bill entered, he was taken to the Kornakova family box by an usher and was greeted by Marina and Andrey who introduced him to Olga's grandma and an array of family cousins.

The weather was perfect and the city of Kostroma had brought in their landscaping crews to cover the grounds with an array of annuals including pansies, begonias, day lilies, and impatiens. It was truly a setting fit for a queen. And now the hour had arrived as the hundreds of guests took their seats in the spacious garden. Now the bride and groom appeared, Olga in her satin gown and lace veil and her trailing train gave an aura reminiscent of a Greek Goddess because she was more beautiful than any mere earthling. Ben Stevens, beside her with his 6ft 4in frame and chiseled body, made them the perfect pair.

Standing beside them at the podium was best man Vadim Matei of Moldova, and maid of honor Alexsandra Dimova of Bulgaria. The priest blessed the rings with a short prayer, placing her ring in his right hand, and his ring in her right hand. Placing the rings on their fingers would have to be delayed until the civil ceremony the next day. A Russian woman read a poem by Alexander Pushkin, and one of Ben Steven's CIA colleagues read a selection by America's beloved Robert Frost. They were then followed by three tenors singing "Russia, My Russia," and "America the Beautiful."

The ceremony ended with the groom kissing the bride, then sweeping her off her feet and carrying her off as if he were taking her to the honeymoon suite. As the band played festive songs, the hundreds of attendees formed a long circular line, kicking their right feet into the air, followed quickly by a kick of their left feet.

Olga and Ben circulated among the crowd, and Bill understood that their time was limited. He gave Olga a hug, then shook hands with Ben, wishing them well. He then moved away quickly before a wave of sentiment kicked in. It was no time for tears. The assembled crowd lined up for the traditional Russian feast, with the thirty-one CIA and RIS members doing the duties as servers.

Darkness had now intervened, and the candles that had been placed around this four acre piece of hallowed ground now signaled that it was time for everyone to shake hands and do their hugs to commemorate a truly special day. Though it was late, Princess was waiting outside to take him back to his hotel. When he got back to his room, he realized that the woman he cared so much about now belonged exclusively to Ben Stevens. They would be living in Easton, and he in St. Petersburg and he wondered if he would ever see her again.

The next day, the civil ceremony took place at the Dept. Of Public Services, which is known as "rospis v zagse" where the couple is greeted by family members with bread and salt. The ceremony lasted about twenty minutes during which time the rings were exchanged and the couple is pronounced man and wife. The parents of the bride, Marina and Andrey then offered the couple two crystal glasses which they were asked to break on the specified brick floor. The more chards of glass, the greater number of years of happiness. Then they went outside and released two white doves into the air for all to see.

Following the ceremony, the newlyweds and their two witnesses traveled around the city in a limousine to visit various historical sites where photographers are waiting to take pictures. Now the wedding is complete but the festivities are not over. The town had erected a huge stage in the shadow of Susanin's statue where the 32 CIA and RIS representatives gathered to let the world know that the hostilities between them were ending and their cooperation to root out the vestiges of terrorism would begin. Ben Stevens delivered the keynote speech and the assembled crowd numbering in the thousands interrupted numerous times to give him a rousing ovation. The city had not seen a celebration of this magnitude since the end of the Great Patriotic War.

The next day, Princess took Bill to the train depot where he would go to Yaroslavi and catch a flight to St. Petersburg. During the flight and taxi ride to his flat, he began to think how lucky he was to have known so many beautiful Russian ladies. For an old guy who started it all by taking advice from a magazine article to, "Don't be afraid to flirt with the ladies if you want a more interesting retirement," it was an adventure that was not possible but Bill knew it was, because he'd lived it.

Since Bill first arrived in St. Petersburg in the spring of 2014 to be with Vera, he had never traveled beyond the city limits except his just ended trip to Kostroma. Of course, there was his house arrest in Chelyabinsk. The train ride back through Kazan enabled him to spend an hour or so around the train depot while the locomotive took on fuel whetted his appetite to visit the city again.

He decided to use Russia's extensive transportation system to not only re-visit Kazan but other cities like Nizhny-Novgorad (Gorky) Smolensk, Samara, Novosibirsk, and even Lenin's hometown of Simbirsk. He also would travel to Tambov and Michurinsk, the home cities of Svetlani Cheranova and Dasha Brumel. From 2018 to 2022, he lived the life of a vagabond, except he had the necessary funds where he could spend up to a month in each of the cities he visited. He would always return to St. Petersburg to recharge his batteries. He had hardly heard from Dasha over this period of time but in a recent short letter she revealed she had been dating a wonderful guy for about a year and maybe she would give some thought to marriage. She had received another promotion and was now in Moscow as Commander of the RIS there. He also received a letter from his tenant in Delmarva that she was retiring and going back to her hometown of Pittsburgh to keep track of her hometown teams, the Steelers, Penguins and Pirates. Bill remembered she had told him she was a big sports fan when she signed the two year lease in 2014. Every two years after she would renew and had never missed a monthly payment in the eight years she had lived there. It was now time to give serious thought to returning to the USA. His lease on his flat was also ending at the end of the month with a hefty increase expected, so he gave notice this would be his last month.

Back to the USA

Leaving St. Petersburg would not be an easy thing to do. Yes, Bill had mostly been on the road visiting other Russian cities, towns and even a few villages but he always looked forward to coming back to his neighborhood where he could reconnect with all those people he cared so much about. His efforts to meet Vera's son Sergey had not been successful since his job took him out of the country. He was now an executive for a giant Russian oil and gas company and although he would come to St. Petersburg on short visits, it was always when Bill was out of town. He had gotten a recent letter from Olga and she now had two daughters, Marina, now five years old and Anastasia, three. He would have to live in his old Delmarva home for an extended period of time until he could clear his mind and figure out where he would spend the final years of his life.

Although it would only be a 90 minute car ride from his home to where Olga lived in Easton, he decided not to tell her he had moved back to the United States. He had not seen her since her wedding and thought it best to not interfere in her family life because the memories of their time together might reignite the flame and that would not be good for either of them.

The day for Bill's trip back to the USA had now arrived and as Arno drove him to the Pulkova Airport where he would board an Aeroflot plane the sadness began to set in. Passing the hospital where Vera spent her last several days took all the intestinal fortitude he could muster from having an emotional breakdown. When they arrived at Pulkova he and Arno hugged and shook hands for what would be the last time. Arno had always been there for him to take him shopping or just ride around the city, and Bill rewarded him with a nice bonus for all his efforts.

He was now on the plane for the 13 hour flight to Washington and he was fortunate to have a seat next to a mature, well educated, and interesting American citizen from Richmond, Virginia by the name of Joanne White. She was an employee of the Virginia State Agricultural Department and had lived in Russia for two years teaching Russian farmers how to attain better yields from their crops. It was interesting that she spent some time at the Michurinsk State Agricultural University where Dasha Brumel spent a year before becoming an RIS trainee.

Bill decided not to mention Dasha since she was such an important official now where Ms. White might think he was trying to impress her. Needless to say, the flight went by quickly and when they de-boarded the plane, they exchanged pleasantries and Bill promised to try to get to the next annual Virginia State Agriculture exhibition in Richmond.

When Bill arrived at his home in Delmarva, his tenant had just moved out the day before and left everything in excellent condition. The old shed and gazebo were still in pretty good shape and even the raised garden where he mostly planted tomatoes needed little work for a spring planting. He doubted very much whether many of his old neighbors were still living here.

He had heard from his tenant that the real estate market had been red hot for several years and most who had sold in the last few years made a tidy profit. He decided he would not allow his age to stop him from doing the things he enjoyed so since it was late April, he would go out and purchase fertilizer for the garden and groceries. While walking the aisles of the local grocery store, he came upon a beautiful lady whose dimples made her identity unmistakable. She had to be Shannon, the young lady who worked at the deli where he enjoyed so many delicious breakfasts when he arrived on the Peninsula. It had been 10 years since he had last seen her but almost instinctively, they hugged because they had developed a respectful and meaningful friendship in the years prior to Bill moving to Russia.

There was so much they wanted to talk about but in the aisle of a grocery store was not the best place so they decided to meet at McDonald's in three hours where they could talk without having to rush. It was ironic that the Deli was where Bill first started his flirting some 16 years earlier. Bill arrived at McDonalds a little early and chose a booth that would give them a little privacy.

When she arrived, they gave each other another hug and she began to relate what had transpired in her life and at the Deli over the intervening years. She was now co-owner of the Deli with her good friend Jennifer and their two boys Nathan and Eric John worked there as bus boys. It would be a great way for young people to earn some spending money with the added benefit of being a good training ground for whatever they chose to do later in life. Julie and Cheryl were still working there but on a reduced schedule.

His special lady, Anita, was now living in Florida with her parents who had moved there permanently about four years ago. Both Bill and Shannon were Pittsburgh Steelers fans having won two more Super Bowls in the years he was away and now had eight titles, two more than the 49ers and Cowboys. When they parted, Bill assured Shannon he would be seeing her on a regular basis as long as he was living in his present home. Seeing and talking to her was very uplifting since up to now, he had not run into any neighbors he knew. They didn't discuss anything about their families or personal lives because sometimes, these can be sensitive matters best not mentioned.

The next several weeks, Bill attended to all his spring time chores, getting his garden ready for his beefy boy and beef master tomatoes, fertilizing his lawn, cutting back his bushes and putting in his annuals. He made his regular trips to the Deli to visit Shannon and Jennifer and a new lady from Belarus named Victoria. It was like having a little bit of Russia in his life.

Susann Tate Enters Bill's Life

Every two weeks, he would make the 90 minute drive to Chincoteague to visit the beach, the lighthouse, Maria's, and walk the miles of nature trails. It was hard to believe that over 10 years had gone by since he and Olga made their regular weekly trips here and his memories of those days were both haunting and precious. He was beginning to love the island and if he didn't return to St. Petersburg, this is where he wanted to finish his final years. Each trip here, he would look over the real estate sales and leases to get some idea on style and price that would fit his requirements.

On his return trip back to Delmarva, he began to think that the five bedroom house was a little much for an old bachelor like him. It was now mid-July and his tomatoes were coming on like gangbusters. Those tomato and bacon sandwiches on homemade bread were always his favorite and he got his fill of them. He would sit out every morning in his gazebo watching the sun rise over the eastern skies while listening to his favorite instrumentals and although he was enjoying his time here, Russia was strong on his mind. But realistically, he understood that at his advanced age, it would not be the practical thing to do.

He looked at his calendar and tomorrow would be the 29th of July. It was an important day because it was Betsy's birthday and he decided to visit the real estate office where Betsy had worked for many years to see if he could talk to an agent about the prospect of placing his home on the market. The next morning, he drove to the building where Betsy was employed but the name had been changed to Miller-Tate Realty.

Nevertheless, he decided to knock on the door. It was just 9am when a handsome lady with dark hair who introduced herself as Susann welcomed him in. She reminded him of a beautiful Persian lady he had known years earlier with a similar name, although the spelling was different. After Bill stated his intention of placing his house on the market, she responded by asking him a question he was sure all agents are trained to ask, "Why did you choose us?" He explained that a lady by the name of Betsy Bond who was very dear to his heart was employed at this location for many years and he felt an obligation to come here at least initially.

From the look on her face, it was obvious that this revelation took her by complete surprise. Almost immediately, she went into this oration of how she had heard of Betsy from the previous owners. As a matter of fact, when her brother-in-law purchased the business, they had been told that she was the model that all agents should try to emulate. Not only for her competence and hard work but she was a pillar in the community, doing volunteer work for every conceivable good cause. Susann went on to say that although she had never met Betsy, she would strive to measure up to her high standards.

With that, Bill had no doubt that he wanted Susann to be his agent if she would accept him and she responded by saying she would be honored to do so. She went on to say that under the new rules, there would be a three day waiting period before any papers could be signed but she could visit his property and give him some idea of what other properties in the neighborhood were selling for. He agreed it would be a good idea and as she walked him to the door, his propensity to flirt had never waned, "Is there a chance you could join me for dinner tonight at Fresco's?" Without hesitation, she agreed saying she loved the restaurant and since it was only a ten minute drive from her townhouse, she would meet him at whatever time he specified. They agreed on 7pm and as he drove away, he began to hum "happy days are here again." He was certain he had met a special lady and he couldn't wait for the evening to arrive.

He went back to doing chores at the house to pass the time and since it was hot, he decided he would wear the new seersucker shirt and trousers he had just purchased the day before.

When he arrived at Fresco's she was sitting on the veranda in a black and white one piece summer dress and she looked spectacular. She said she arrived 15 minutes early because she had been looking forward to the evening and her anxiety got the best of her. This really lifted his spirits because it gave him a feeling she really wanted to be here instead of treating it as a duty to a future client.

Her dress had accentuated all her natural assets and already his imagination was getting way ahead of where it should be at this stage of their friendship. As a matter of fact, it was awful for him to think of her in that way but it was in his DNA because he had always been enamored by women of great beauty and charm and she would not take a back seat to anyone in that department. Of course, he had just met her this morning and for him to form an opinion already was premature but he was certain she was everything he imagined. They both ordered creamy crab soup for an appetizer and decided to order two entrees sharing with each other. One was a veal salmon combo prepared in a sauce that was as delicious as either could remember and the second entrée was broiled rockfish stuffed with their incomparable crab imperial. Their wine selection was a bordeau and it more than fit the bill.

They finished with a cup of tea and some homemade bread pudding and it was a meal worth remembering. Their conversation touched on some of their past with her explaining that she was a 53 year old widow although she seemed reluctant to tell him what had happened to her husband and of course, it would have been uncouth of him to ask. She seemed anxious to hear about the years he had spent living in Russia.

He decided not to mention Olga or Dasha or his time under house arrest in Chelyabinsk but did reveal that he had fallen in love with Vera Petrova and had gone to St. Petersburg with the intention of marrying her. He went on to explain about her van accident and her subsequent death several days later. Maybe he should not have told

Susann because she seemed to be genuinely moved since she could see it was an emotional moment for him.

He changed the subject quickly to what an enjoyable evening it had been and as he walked her to her car, they agreed to meet the next day at 10am at his house at which time she would make an assessment in regards to the value of his property and the price he should consider asking.

After driving just five minutes up the road, he realized that his feelings were way too strong. He felt ashamed that he was thinking about her in a physical way after knowing her for less than a day. Besides, he was over three decades older and he was sure if she shared a bed with a man, it would be with some prospect of getting married. Of course, he had no idea how much time had elapsed since she lost her spouse so it was almost ludicrous to have these thoughts in his mind. But regardless of his feelings for her, he was confident he had chosen the right person to handle any transaction regarding the sale of his house and property.

When Susann arrived the next day, she was just as stunning as the night before with a light summer dress of blue and white again bringing out all her natural beauty. After she looked over the property, they sat in his gazebo and she began to show him what other properties of similar style were selling for and she suggested he should ask for at least a twenty thousand dollar premium over the others because of his superior lot. When she wrote down the number, she thought he should ask, he was more than satisfied. She went on to say she didn't think it would take over three months to do the deal. That meant he would have to be out by the first of November so he would have to act quickly to either lease or purchase a property in Chincoteague. One thing he was certain of, since this would be off season there he could at least obtain a short lease at a bargain price. So now when the three day mandatory time was over, she could get the paper work started. By now, she had sensed that Bill had developed a crush and she seemed to enjoy the interest by giving him a flirtatious smile and wink.

When she left, she said she would call him in a couple days when the papers were ready and they could meet at her office or she would be happy to come over to his dining room table to explain everything and he could sign if he was satisfied that the paperwork was in order. Without really thinking, he said he would prefer her coming to his house since his mind always worked better in a familiar setting. With that, she smiled and gave him another wink, knowing what his choice would be. As they walked to her car, they shook hands and this time he gave her a kiss on her cheek which she seemed to be very comfortable with.

When Susann said she didn't think it would take over three months to sell his house, he knew he had to act quickly to find another place to live. It was not practical to think of moving back to St. Petersburg at his age so he decided that Chincoteague would probably be his best choice. Since it would take a few days to get the paperwork ready, he would drive down in the morning for a two day stay and check out the real estate market there. When he arrived there, he went over to the location where he and Svetlani stayed over a decade earlier. He preferred the rustic cabins instead of the rooms at the seedy motels, especially during the high season when not as much care is taken to clean up after previous guests checked out. As luck would have it, he was not only able to secure a cabin but the very one he shared with Svetlani.

After checking in, Bill visited several real estate offices on the island. He followed the map the realtors gave him to all the ones he thought might fit his needs but after a day up and down the streets he had not found the one suitable for an old bachelor. By this time, he was hungry so he sauntered over to a cookout being sponsored by the Chamber of Commerce and got his fill of chicken and oysters. To provide a nice ambiance, there was a performer with his guitar singing songs like, "Its Five O'clock somewhere." And it was appropriate because this was exactly what the time was here.

After his fill of good food, he decided to go over to his cabin to rest a while, but somehow he made a turn up a narrow road that was almost unnoticeable unless you knew it was there. After proceeding about 300 yards, it was as if providence had led him here. There in the perfectly manicured lawn, a sign was posted, "For sale or lease by owner." It took Bill less than a minute to write down the telephone number listed and the house from the outside looked perfect for his needs. It was a Cape Cod and it was obvious that great thought had been given to its construction with a deep pitched roof with a long overhang to guard against the fierce ocean winds… an ocean just a few miles away. He guessed the house was about 30 years old and the wood shingles on the roof and clapboard siding were still in excellent condition. It was evident that the house and property had been well maintained by the owners. Just as he was driving away, a young couple pulled into the driveway and asked, "Would you like to take a look inside?"

He could not resist the offer, "Yes if you don't think the owners would mind." They went on to say they had just gotten married a few days ago and were renting the house for a week. They assured him the owners would appreciate them showing the property to any prospective buyer.

The main room took his eye as soon as he entered. A cast-iron stove in the middle for wood burning was the perfect centerpiece. The wood log walls, obviously hewed from the local pine stock gave you a feeling of comfort and warmth. Before looking further, Bill instinctively knew this was the place he wanted to spend his remaining years. There was a master bedroom and two smaller ones with two baths.

In the back, was a nice sized deck shaped like a fishing boat with benches on the inside perimeter. It would be perfect for bird watching and cookouts. Anxious to go back to his cabin and call the owners, he thanked the honeymooners and wished them a long happy life together. When he arrived back to his cabin, he called the number he had written down from the posted sign and was lucky enough to speak to one of the owners and she identified herself as Elaine Oaks.

After just a few minutes into their conversation, Bill was impressed with her sincerity and poise. She also had a great sense of humor because when he asked her the asking price, without hesitation, she responded, "One million, six hundred thousand and fifty dollars." It almost took his breath away at first but when she added the fifty dollars at the end, he understood she was just joking. He told her that was a little more than he could afford she told him the price was actually less than $500,000. He thought it was a fair price and he was not about to try to talk the price down, especially during these good times.

Elaine went on to explain that they lived in Arlington, Virginia and that her husband Richard who was employed as an engineer for a defense contractor was being transferred to California. They were both in love with their house because they had used it as a getaway from the hectic pace in the Washington area on weekends and vacations. He told her he had fallen in love with her house and explained his situation with his property in Delmarva and told her he would be willing to pay cash if she and her husband would agree to a Nov. 1 settlement date. He explained that even if his house had not settled by then, he had sufficient assets to assure her the cash would be put in an escrow account in her and Richards name by then. Bill also offered to lease the property for the entire month of October if she had not yet had renters for that month. She said she would discuss his offer in its entirety with her husband and she was sure he would look favorably on his proposal. They ended their conversation in a spirit of trust, agreeing to keep in touch either by phone or e-mail.

As Bill lay down in his cabin that evening, he couldn't be happier. Things were moving in his direction at a quick pace and his conversation with Elaine Oaks gave him a feeling of great satisfaction because she had given him confidence that he was dealing with honest, trustworthy people and he believed she felt the same way about him.

When he awoke the next morning to get his shower, he could not help but to think that he and Svetlani were soaping each other down in this very place those many years ago. For sure, it had gone through some renovation since then with a modern showerhead with new tile floor and walls, but the fact that they had shared the same place was a time worth remembering.

When he got dressed and went outside, it was going to be a Chamber of Commerce Day, not a cloud to be seen and for the first of August, a delightful 80 degree day. Before driving back to Delmarva, Bill stopped at the local McDonalds and had a sausage biscuit before heading for the beach to sit and watch the many beach goers enjoying their time at this special piece of property on the Atlantic Ocean. Of course, he would never forget his many trips here with Olga so many years ago and their narrow escape from death. He wondered since she only lived a few hours away in Easton whether she would visit here with her husband Ben and their two children, Marina and Anastasia.

Wouldn't it be ironic if she was to appear at this very moment and if so, he would have a lot of explaining to do since she believed he was still in Russia. His two day visit here was certainly a fruitful one and now it was time to drive back to Delmarva because Susann would be coming to his house tomorrow to go over all the paperwork regarding the pending sale of his house. It was funny that he did not know her last name as yet. There was little doubt she had probably mentioned it to him a few times but he was so enamored by her extraordinary beauty that his mind was wondering about other things at those times.

When he got home that evening, he went to the Miller-Tate website to get a list of their agents and there was her name, Susann Tate. She had told him that her brother-in-law had purchased the business from the original owners and now this made sense since her late husband was the brother of the new owner. Why the Miller part in the firm's name was there, he didn't know but he guessed at some time down the road, he would learn. He had received an e-mail from her saying all the paperwork pertaining to the sale of his house and property was complete and if it was okay with him, she would come by tomorrow at 10am to secure his signature and bring by the lawn sign to place in his front yard. She went on to say that a very nice couple had visited their offices the day before looking for a particular style of house in a nice neighborhood no further than two miles from the beach. They preferred not to be any closer either to avoid all the noise and traffic associated with the beach goers. She told them about his property being available in a day or so and they seemed anxious to look at it as soon as possible. I told them I would check with you when we met in the morning and if you agreed, they would love to come by tomorrow afternoon.

Wow!!!! It was all happening so fast his mind could not absorb it all. He was tired from his two day visit to Chincoteague but his immediate inclination was to tell them yes of course, let them come by. He was sure he had sealed the deal with Elaine Oaks for the property in Chincoteague and he was anxious to move there as soon as possible.

When Susann arrived at Bill's house the next morning at 10am sharp, she was dressed to kill. She was very impressive the evening they dined together at Fresco's but some people might think her dress today was designed to seduce. Her makeup made her lips appear fuller and when he opened the door to let her in the perfume reminded him of the scent Olga had chosen so many years ago at the Quality Inn. It was intoxicating then and it had the same effect now. The only thing he could conclude was that she had some special place to go after her meeting with him. They shook hands and Bill gave her a light kiss on the cheek each expressing their greetings that it was nice to see each other again. Bill had cleared the dining room table and told her to feel free to place her briefcase there and make herself at home.

He had made some coffee and also had some cookies and orange juice on hand. He had complete faith that the paperwork she had prepared was more than proper so when she explained it all to him, it was almost like he didn't hear a word although he pretended to listen carefully. Their chairs were close together and every now and then, her hand would pat him on the knee when she was trying to make a strong point. It was a good way of getting his attention and whether she meant for him to reciprocate in some way he didn't know, but he didn't want to take the chance for fear of losing someone he really respected. He had known ladies in the past that would touch in a similar way but they were just trying to accentuate their exuberance in what they were trying to convey. It was easy to notice that she was energized and seemed anxious to tell Bill about the couple who had visited her office.

She explained that they lived in Wilmington, Delaware and were in the area for two days, "and asked if they could have your address so they could just take a drive through your neighborhood and get a peek of your house from the outside and I saw no harm in doing so. They sent me an e-mail early this morning, expressing how much they loved everything they observed and wondered if they could drop by this afternoon about 2pm to see inside the house."

"Of course let them come by"… he hoped that they would not notice his old furniture because he had already donated all of it to the Salvation Army.

With that, it was now time to put his "John Hancock" on all the documents, after which she had more she wanted to discuss with him. "Bill I dressed this way in hopes I could lure you to go to dinner this evening with me. I will be happy to do the 2pm walk through with the Casey`s if you would rather not be here. When they leave, it will be important for us to talk about the logistics and possible dates for settlement if you accept the conditions of the provisional contract I will write for them today. I have brought the yard sign for your front lawn and I can place it there now or maybe it would be better to wait until after the Casey's are gone. It may not be necessary to even place one if everything goes as I anticipate."

And now it was Bill's turn to respond to all that had been presented to him by first accepting her dinner invitation for this evening. He further conveyed to her how much he appreciated the effort she had given to his project and expressed his full confidence in her to proceed on the expedited schedule they were now on. His desire was to leave everything up to her regarding the time they would be here giving him the opportunity to do some shopping. They would meet at 7pm at Schooners for dinner.

It was noon and Susann said she would take the signed documents back to her office and while there, pick up a provisional contract for the Casey's to sign if they were so inclined. They would still have the five day "right of recission" giving them time to be sure they did not suffer from "buyer's remorse." She said she would return at 1:45pm to meet the Casey's at which time Bill gave her the key to his house.

When he returned home about 5pm, Susann had left a note that Robert and Betty Casey were extremely happy with everything and were eager to sign the provisional contract. When he arrived at Schooners she was early as usual and now she had changed again into another dress that was just as provocative as the one she had worn this morning for their 10am meeting. When they sat down, they both ordered the prime rib and ribs buffet and frozen margaritas. She wanted to tell him a little more about the Casey's. They were both chemical engineers employed by DuPont Company in Wilmington. They had invested their money well over the years and now wanted to use their hard earned earnings to get a place close to the beach. The settlement would be easy since they would be paying in cash. They agreed on a settlement date of Sept. 28. Now she wanted to tell him how she lost her husband. "It was the summer of 2017, just over five years ago and we lived in Annapolis in an expensive home on the Severn River. John and I were very happy and we owned a small investment business that was doing exceptionally well."

"At first, we were just a two person operation but when our business expanded, we needed more help and we hired this young lady just out of the University of Maryland business school. She was an excellent employee on salary and always gave more hours than was required, coming in early and leaving late. She was not only great in the office but also in the bedroom as my husband found out and although I suspected they were having an affair I was never in a position to prove it but both were found dead in a seedy motel in Hagerstown, Md."

"Their nude bodies were taken to the morgue and it was determined they died of asphyxiation but the medical examiners were never able to ascertain what actually killed them. It was summertime so there was no malfunctioning heater. There were no marks on either of their throats that would suggest strangulation. Their blood tests showed a high level of carbon dioxide but they were never able to learn its origin. To this day, the case remains unsolved. Well Bill, this is the story and I am glad I got it off my chest. I hope you will not repeat it to anyone else."

He was stunned to hear this from a woman he respected and cared about so much and promised not to utter a word to anyone. She was truly an amazing woman because she was not only able to overcome this tragedy, but she seemed to have thrived because of it. She was a confident, strong and determined woman and was beautiful in every meaning of the word. Today, in his dining room, she was not afraid to flirt a little and the way she dressed proved she was not afraid to display her sexuality and that was good.

As they walked toward her car, they agreed to get back together in the coming week to go over any remaining business regarding the sale of his home. On the drive back home, all he could think about was the sad events regarding Susann's husband. He had endured much over the last 12 years losing Vera and all the rest but he had time to heal. Yet, in her case, until the mystery was solved on how John and his lover died there would always be suspicious minds.

Over the next few weeks, Bill and Susann got together on several occasions for lunch and he told her the story of how he had lost Vera. They had become good friends and he was going to miss her when he moved to Chincoteague. Of course, it was only a 90 minute drive so he could always return to visit her, Shannon, Jennifer, Julie, and Cheryl and a few others whose friendship he valued. He was living in an empty house now, the Salvation Army had taken his furniture and the cleaning crew he hired did a great job in getting it spic and span for the new owners. Sept. 28th had arrived and he would get to meet the new owners, Robert and Betty Casey because this was settlement day. Bill packed up his clothes and computer in his sand-mobile and headed for the offices of Miller-Tate Realty. He had never learned where the Miller came from but sometimes, it is better not to know everything.

After meeting the Casey's he was happy because he knew they would be people the community would embrace. They were young and vibrant and from the looks of their bodies, it was apparent they were health nuts and any neighborhood always benefits from an infusion of vitality. They shook hands and now it was time for Bill to get in his sand-mobile and head for his new home. Susann came out to say goodbye and they embraced for what seemed like several minutes but yet there were no tears because they knew they were within two hours of each other. On the drive down, his mind had shifted to his new life in Chincoteague. The money from the sale of his house was now in the bank and he would stop and transfer the full amount he would pay to Richard and Elaine Oaks on Oct. 1. Since this was a deal strictly between him and them, the entire transaction could be handled via electronic mail transfers and Federal Express.

Olga and Bill Reunite in Chincoteague

When Bill arrived at his new home, the last renters were just moving out and they left everything in excellent condition and although he was a day early, he now considered himself an official resident of Chincoteague. For now, he could get along fine with the furniture there but in a day or so, he would have to go to the local furniture outlet to purchase a new lounge chair and mattress. If you love the fall of the year, this is the place to be. The best way to travel around town is by motor scooter and he found a used one in a yard sale on Church Street that fit his needs perfectly. Bill was an outgoing guy and it didn't take him long to meet some of the permanent residents there.

The next several months, the town would be hopping with events such as, The Annual Chincoteague Oyster Festival; The Annual Tree Lighting Ceremony; The Annual Chili and Chowder Cook-off; and The Annual Christmas Parade. It was a great time to be here and although the weather was turning cold, it was pure joy to put a few logs in his cast iron stove and sit next to it in his new lounge chair with some hot chocolate and a good book.

When Bill was living in Russia, he would travel to the various towns and cities using their extensive railroad system. Although there were few passenger rail services here, he could drive to places like Norfolk, Charleston and Savannah and his intention was to do so. It was football and hockey season and his television packages allowed him to watch all the games of interest to him.

When spring arrived, he would be taking fishing trips out of towns like Crisfield, Cape Charles and Pocomoke City. There were no women in his life now but knowing that Olga and Susann were close gave him a feeling of contentment. Olga still believed he was living in St. Petersburg and he wanted to keep it that way at least for now. Yes, there were times when he felt a little lonely but the best way to deal with it was to drive to Easton now and then to be close to Olga. He never quite had the courage to drive down the street where she lived. He remembered taking her there when she was released by the CIA back many years ago during the prisoner exchange program. How could he forget that day because he remembered stopping just a few miles before he was to meet Ben where they parked and bid farewell with hugs and kisses?

Their wedding a few years later in Kostroma and the great event that followed was both memorable and historic. Maybe if she saw him now, she wouldn't recognize him. Every time he drove to Easton, he would continue on to St. Michaels because he was fond of historic old towns whether here or in Russia. The cafés along the waterfront were known for their delicious oyster and potato salad dishes and he always got his fill when visiting here.

He never let any grass grow under his feet over the next couple of years, visiting Pittsburgh on several occasions to watch the Steelers and Penguins. Traveling to Charleston to see all the antebellum homes and civil war relics like the hulk of the H.L. Hunley submarine and to Savannah to visit the historic places especially along the waterfront of the Savannah River was just a sampling of his travels during the off season in Chincoteague although in reality, there was always something going on here even in the dead of winter. Besides, he loved sitting in his lounge chair next to his cast iron stove when the winter winds were blowing the clapboard siding on his Cape Cod.

It was a good time for reading old books he never had the time for in the past. Tonight, his selection would be 50 Shades of Grey. It wasn't a book he would recommend to the average reader. Bondage, submission and sadism had never appealed to him as necessary props since the female body with all its heavenly places to go was more than he ever needed or wanted to get his juices flowing. In fact, just lying in bed cuddled up next to a woman with his head on her breasts and his hand on her vulva was all he ever wanted at times.

Nevertheless, the two characters in the book, a college student, Anastasia Steele and business man, Christian Grey reminded him of the time when he was a young 25 year old business man going with an 18 year old beautiful red haired girl who was a college freshman at the University of Virginia Medical School. She was more interested in collecting his sperm to study under a microscope but she used conventional methods and just at that moment, she had a small glass container to collect most of it although on occasion, it got a little messy.

It was now the winter of 2023-24 and Bill's life at Chincoteague was better than he ever imagined now taking the fishing trips out of Crisfield on a regular basis when the weather would permit. Although there were times when his age reminded him he could not perform certain tasks such as putting up a heavy ladder to check his roof shingles, his overall mobility was good. It was now late March and he had signed up with a group out of Salisbury to take a one week trip to Cancun, Mexico from the local airport.

He didn't know any of his fellow travelers personally but just lying on the warm beach and ordering margaritas from the beachside stands was a good way to get tuned up for all the springtime activities that would soon be in full swing in Chincoteague. Making the island his home base and traveling to different venues was a much better lifestyle than going to Florida. When he got back home, spring had arrived in all its glory. As an early warm breeze filtered its way onto his back deck, he could see the trees and bushes already in the beginning stages of their blooming period and it was good to be alive.

He had slept in and it was nearly 10am when he opened his front shutters and noticed a black sports car entering his driveway. He couldn't remember anyone he knew with this kind of car. Maybe it was Suzann Tate, but she was not the type to visit without giving him some notice.

When the driver side door opened, he could not believe his eyes. He had not seen her since her wedding nearly eight years ago but her features were unmistakable and she was as spectacular as ever. But how did she find him? As far as she knew, he was still living in St. Petersburg but as she walked up the steps, he opened the door and there she stood. It was Olga and tears were flowing profusely from both as they embraced tightly, neither wanting to let go. They were both feeling every emotion possible because so much had transpired between them since the time she first appeared at his table at Hannah's in the summer of 2010.

She was twenty-three then and doing some quick math, she would be 38 in November of this year. He led her over to a comfortable chair and he got some paper tissue for both, although the tears had now given way to smiles.

Finally, she spoke her first words, "I should be very angry with you for not telling me you had moved from St. Petersburg to here but I will save my admonishment until later. The years have treated you well Bill. Are you happy?"

"Yes, I have been staying very busy with my traveling, fishing and all the activities on the island and I still get great pleasure out of going to the beach to watch the ladies in their bikinis, but I am more interested in your life. How are Ben, Marina and Anastasia?" At first, she seemed hesitant to answer his question and yet it was apparent that the question he posed had hit a raw nerve and she seemed anxious to get something off her chest so to speak when, "Ben took Marina and Anastasia to Disney World for a few days to give me a break. Our marriage and family life had been going well until six months ago when I discovered he had been seeing another woman in Washington, D.C."

"Can I Stay with You Tonight?"

Olga continued, "Ben had to attend meetings there at the Pentagon regarding his job at the CIA every three months. It was a Homeland Security thing where representatives from the CIA, the FBI, the NSA and the Defense Department get together to coordinate their efforts in their continuing war against world terrorism. As I understand it, the Pentagon complex of buildings are swarming with attractive young ladies and several of them made a play for him. He resisted their advances at first but finally he gave into one of them and now he seems to be unwilling to end their six month affair, meeting in Annapolis on a regular basis to exchange body fluids."

At this time, the tears were flowing from her eyes and Bill took some more tissues and wiped them away, hugging her at the same time. She continued, "I hope our marriage will survive for the sake of the kids. Marina and Anastasia love our neighborhood and schools and to disrupt their lives in their formative years would be difficult for them."

Bill was stunned by all these revelations when he suggested that since it was such a beautiful day, why not go over to the beach for the afternoon and she responded, "I would love to." Olga went to her car and brought in her travel bag and asked him if she could use one of his bedrooms to change into some appropriate beachwear and he gave her an enthusiastic "thumbs up." When she came out of the bedroom, Bill could not believe that Ben could even look at another woman after seeing her. She was beautiful beyond description. The beachwear she had chosen left little for the imagination and even at his advanced age, he was feeling expansion in all the right places. He wanted so much to direct her back to the bedroom and kiss and caress her from head to toe as he had done before so many years ago but it wasn't his call. "How do I look?" And Bill could not help but to respond, "There are no words adequate enough to describe your beauty."

With that, she came closer and kissed him on the lips and suggested that maybe it would be a good time to go get some lunch and then go to the beach. They loaded up his sand-mobile this time with his beach umbrella along with some chairs and towels. They first stopped at the Sea-Shell Grille to have a sandwich and juice and then proceeded toward the beach. On the way, she wanted to stop at the bottom of the hill and walk up the path leading to the old lighthouse they both knew so well. They stood on what they guessed was the very place where his sand-mobile was parked on that fateful day. How could he ever forget her words that day when he offered to button her blouse, "Not just yet Bill, they are yours." And now here they stood 14 years later and she is even more beautiful now at age 38. After about 20 minutes on the hill that saved their lives, they headed for the beach. This time, she wanted to be far removed from the location where she set up her transponder and transmitters back in 2010. She wanted no reminders of her days in the RIS although their mission today is quite different from what it was then. As they sat on their chairs facing the Atlantic Ocean, the southern sun warmed their bodies and he was as proud as could be because he had the sexiest woman on the planet sitting next to him.

Olga took Bill's hand as if to say, "I need your calm and upbeat spirit because I have come to a crossroad in my life and what direction it takes me is unknown and scary. And Bill took her hand as if to say I will be here as long as you need me. All of a sudden, she came out of her chair and said, "I am going to build you a sandcastle." As she began to move piles of sand to begin her project two young girls about age eight came over to lend her their plastic shovels and they would be her helpers.

She explained that she was building the St. Michaels Castle located in St. Petersburg, Russia and as it began to take shape and gain a personality, other beach goers came over to marvel at how many details she was able to include with just loose sand. And when the masterpiece was complete, she got a rousing ovation from all. There was little doubt that she was feeling buoyant from her beach experience because before getting in his sand-mobile for the short trip back to his Cape Cod, she put her arms around him and gave him a very affectionate hug. As they travelled on the same road they had been on 14 years earlier when it was filling with debris and flooding from the muddy waters, he wondered if that memory was on her mind today or had she been so overwhelmed by everything that had happened subsequently perhaps she had erased it all from her mind.

When they arrived at the ice cream store, she asked Bill to wait inside until she could call Ben and the girls in Florida. After her call, she said the girls were enjoying their time with Mickey Mouse and Donald Duck. She did not mention whether she talked to Ben and naturally he was not going to press the matter. While enjoying their ice cream, he decided to ask her how she found out he was living in Chincoteague.

She said she would not divulge her source but when she had been told Bill had moved from St. Petersburg to Delmarva and then to Chincoteague at first she thought this person was just trying to get a reaction. But when the source insisted it was true, she decided to check the real estate transactions in the county records and sure enough, she found his address. "I know the reason you never told me was because you were afraid you would disrupt our family in some way, but that was not a good reason so I am upset with you." Her last five words were not meant to be serious because then she took his hand and delivered a bombshell, "Bill, I don't want to go home tonight. Can I stay with you until morning?"

Although in a state of disbelief because he was aware of the implications, he responded, "Yes, of course. I have three bedrooms."

"No Bill, I want to be in your bedroom in your bed with you."

Knowing she was probably getting some kind of revenge for Ben, he could not resist her offer. "If it will make you happy, I will be most honored to do so." She was still in her bikini and now his imagination of what was to follow later in the evening was driving him to the brink of anticipation. When they got into his vehicle to drive to his Cape Cod, she suggested that since it was getting close to dinner time, maybe they should clean up first and go out to dinner before retiring for the evening. He had no choice but to agree but he understood her suggestion made sense.

When they arrived, she immediately took the big bathroom and Bill took the smaller one. He took his shower and dressed but she had not yet emerged from the bathroom she claimed and then he heard her voice using her sexy Russian dialect, "Come to the bathroom door for a minute." She was standing there with a towel around her midriff with her breasts fully exposed and asked Bill to come over to caress them and think of them as an appetizer before the entrée later tonight after getting back from dinner. After allowing him a few minutes at breast level, she knelt down and kissed him in a teasing way, pretending to talk to that part of his anatomy, "Don't be in such a hurry, I promise I will take good care of you when we return."

They went to a new restaurant which had just opened last year and had gained a reputation for elegance and fine dining, by the name of Cappy's Seafood and Steak Emporium. The food and service were excellent but the prices were modest when compared to similar type restaurants closer to the big cities and towns. Although its clientele were mainly tourists and military and civilians from the Wallops Island top secret base up the road, it was still an affordable choice for locals as well.

Their specialty was oysters and because of their reputation as an aphrodisiac, just for fun they both settled on the oyster stew, oysters Rockefeller, and oysters on the half shell. A bottle of wine from the local vintner made it all go down so easy and of course the bread pudding was special. The soft music from the great artists of the past like Frank Sinatra and Dean Martin added to the ambiance and if this was a prelude to what was to follow in Bill's bedroom later, it would be an unforgettable experience.

The drive back to his Cape Cod was one of anticipation. The night air had gotten chilly and so when they entered, he threw a few logs in the cast iron stove and within minutes, it was cozy and she was now in her teasing mode, touching him in the most sensitive places and if getting him ready was her goal, he couldn't remember any time in his life when he was more ready than tonight.

Olga disappeared for a few minutes but then he heard her distinctive and sexy Russian voice, "Come into the bedroom, Bill, it is time for me to fulfill my promises to you." When he opened the door, she was lying there with her legs slightly spread, leaving nothing to the imagination, no panties, no bra, as naked as the day she was born. She then reminded him of the time they were in the lobby of the Azimut Hotel in St. Petersburg when he expressed his desire to kiss her from head to toe. "I wanted to give you the opportunity at the time but circumstances intervened and I couldn't make it happen, but I am here for you now."

Bill was trembling and in a state of semi-shock because her nude body was more beautiful and desirable than he had ever dreamed. Yes, she was wearing her bikini today at the beach and that was plenty exciting but now she was offering herself to him in his bed and now he was shaking and was about to have a premature release. She seemed to recognize his dilemma, "Place it on my lips Bill and don't worry, I will be able to get it up for you again later. It has happened many times to Ben in the past and it never spoiled his oral desire for my body."

And it was a gusher he didn't think would be possible for a man his age but the oysters they enjoyed earlier must have had something to do with it. After a short recovery period, he was touching, kissing and caressing her forehead, her nose, her throat, breasts, navel, clitoris, vagina, inner thighs and toes. It was a day and night he would savor for whatever time he had remaining on this earth.

When he awoke the next morning, Olga was gone but she left this note on his door. "My Dear Bill, sorry I had to rush off early this morning but Ben and the girls will be back this afternoon and I have to pick them up from the airport. You were sleeping so soundly, I didn't want to wake you up. Our time together rejuvenated my spirit. I want you to know that you are a very desirable man to be with whether at the beach, for dinner, or in bed. Maybe we can do it again in the future. Whether Ben and I can coexist for the sake of our daughters is still unknown but as of now, he is still seeing his mistress and I am not about to plead with him to give her up. Meanwhile, I will be thinking of you and our wonderful time together and I can't wait for the opportunity to be with you again. Love, Olga."

Farewell

Bill could not remember being this happy in a long time. Yes, he felt guilty in a way because of her family situation but he and Olga had been through so much together. It wasn't about just being in bed with her but to provide the moral and spiritual support she needed when she learned Ben had a mistress.

As spring gave way to summer and then to fall, she would make more visits to Chincoteague and their time in bed was not always their top priority. She wanted to be there to relax and forget her day to day problems and they would walk the trails together hand in hand. The winter of 2024-2025 was turning out to be a rather harsh one and Bill spent most of his time indoors watching all of his favorite sports. The Steelers were doing great and the Penguins were holding their own. On January 7th, he was with Olga celebrating Russian Christmas or Father Frost Day as it is known there. She never mentioned where Ben and the girls were that day and he never asked. It was one of the coldest days on record at 11 below zero and being with her in bed that day provided all the warmth required for their celebration of this Russian holiday. When Olga headed home to Easton that day, Bill was fearful she might get stranded somewhere on the highway and insisted on following her until she got to the city limits.

Several months had passed and it was now late April. The winter was surrendering its icy grip and Bill decided to join a group of fishermen on a fishing trip out of Crisfield.

The six hour scheduled excursion turned out to be an adventure for not only the skipper, but all eight of the fishermen on board. About two hours out the air became cold and the winds picked up and torrents of sleet were making it impossible to see, let alone fish. Trying to rush spring along turned out to be a huge mistake and without the experienced skipper on board, it was doubtful they could have made it into port at all. Although they were three hours late getting there with no fish for their efforts, they were grateful just to be back. When Bill got home, he received an e-mail from Olga reminding him that May 5th was an important day for them and wondering if she could visit him to celebrate. He couldn't remember at first what the significance of that date was but he pretended to remember when he wrote right back saying he would be looking forward to her arrival.

The next day after his fishing trip, he developed a cough and a heavy chest accompanied by the chills and he spent the day in bed, getting up to have some chicken and cabbage soup while taking some over the counter medication. He began to feel better a few days later. But on May 4th, the night before Olga was to arrive, he suffered a relapse with a heavy cough and difficult breathing and he could just barely make it to his lounge chair.

He was too weak to even write Olga to tell her not to come. When she arrived the next morning, she knocked but got no response. Remembering he had told her to come in any time he didn't answer, she removed the key from underneath the flower pot and let herself in. She walked over to his chair and whispered in his ear, "Good morning Bill, it's Olga, it's our day to celebrate." She then kissed his forehead and now it was apparent that he had passed on.

She went over to his computer and penned a letter to Betsy Bond: "You may not remember me but I met you several times back in the summer of 2010 when I worked at Hannah's. My name is Olga Kornakova and I have known Bill for 15 years. Last year, I learned that he had moved from Russia to Chincoteague and I have visited him on several occasions over this past year. We were to have lunch together today but when I knocked, he did not answer. By this time, you have probably figured out that he is no longer with us. On one of my visits, he opened a drawer in his desk and showed me two pint containers of soil, one from the banks of the Volga River in Russia and the other from the banks of the Youghiogheny River in Pennsylvania and asked that his cremated ashes be mixed with them and dispersed in the air on the first windy day in the woods behind the old lighthouse in Chincoteague. I heard from Bill that your health is not so good so if you'd like, I will take on that heavy burden because that hill where the lighthouse stands has a special meaning to me. Love, Olga"

After the autopsy confirmed that Bill had succumbed from viral pneumonia and after a week since his passing, she climbed the hill to the lighthouse, mixed his remains with the pints of soil and waited for a gust of wind and now his days on this earth were over. The same hill that had saved him 15 years earlier had now become his burial place. She walked back down the hill and got in her black sports car and drove away. Whether she and Ben ever worked out their problems was unknown but for the sake of Marina and Anastasia, they owed it to them and each other to give it their best effort.

Epilogue

It was the autumn of 2026 and 16 months had passed since Olga mixed Bill Bond's remains with two pints of soil and dispersed them in the wind behind the Chincoteague Island Lighthouse. Galina, a most stunning Russian woman had met Bill Bond in October of 1982 while visiting her sister in America. They had a brief two week intensive romance and when she returned to Russia she discovered she was carrying his baby. She decided not to tell Bill, and one year after the birth of her son, she met and married Vitali Sokolov, and from that time forward she would be Galina Sokolova and her son would be Vasily Sokolov.

Vitali had passed away two years earlier in 2024 and Galina, now 71 with just several months to live decides to tell Vasily, now 43 that Bill Bond was his biological father, not Vitali as he was led to believe. Vasily becomes a driven man to obtain dual-citizenship and begins a search to learn as much as he can about his birth father and those who knew him.

His efforts, leads him down a path that is so unimaginable, so shocking and at times so sensual that only Jac. K. Spence can make sense of it all.

His follow-up novel will be titled, YELENA, A Story of Unmitigated Love and Passion. Mr. Spence guarantees it will keep you squirming in your seat until the very end.

Phrases

She was still asleep in his arms when he noticed her beach blouse had become unbuttoned and her breasts were within inches of his lips.

When her eyes opened, Bill, being the gentleman as always, "Allow me to button you up." But Olga insisted, "Not just yet Bill, they are yours."

"Can I touch you Bill?" To not know the implications of that simple question would be the height of naivety.

"And Bill, if you get lonely tonight I will be here for you."

"If you decide to sleep in your panties and bra or nothing at all I have no objections."

"Yes, we can go to dinner, but I hope you will show me some respect by not fixating your eyes on every set of breasts like some immature schoolboy."

"I'll hold it for you and then you can hold it for me and don't worry, if it gets a little soft I will get it back up for you. Feel free to guide me and tell me what your desires are."

"Everything that happens in that bed tonight will be therapy we both need."

"Kiss and caress them for me now, they will be an appetizer for later tonight when we return from dinner."

About the Author

Jac. K. Spence decided to write the novel, "Bill and Olga" after receiving an invitation from a dear friend to visit Russia, her home country. His travels through parts of this vast land was the inspiration for turning an idea into a book. Spence, using his imagination began to wonder, "What if his good friend was really a spy for the Russian Intelligence Service"? Female agents, as we learned from Anna Chapman, were expected to use their beauty and body to accomplish their assigned mission. Olga, just 23 years old, and a top graduate of the RIS Training Academy outside of Moscow, pulls Bill into her web of deception and betrayal with precision and guile of a seasoned operative. Bill, now in the autumn of his years is so smitten with her charismatic personality and sex appeal becomes the perfect cover and shill for her clandestine operations. His journey leads him into sensual situations he finds too difficult to resist. Although Bill and Olga's relationship is tumultuous with a high degree of jealousy, betrayal, sex, and intrigue their lives becomes a fifteen year odyssey that neither can ever forget.